"I don't mean you're not a good doctor!"

Plunging her hands into the hot, soapy water, Casey said quickly, "I hope you don't think I meant to imply you weren't giving my aunt adequate care. It's just that—"

"Oh, I understand." Drying a tall iced-tea glass, Travis slanted a wry look at her. "You just don't think a hick doctor who drives a car like mine could possibly handle a fractured leg."

Casey felt flustered. "No, that's not it at all. But my father's very anxious for her to have the best care and— Oh, dear, I don't— It's very hard to argue with my father, you see. He's a man used to giving orders...."

"I suppose you mean he's someone used to power. I've had a little experience with that. Being up against power. That's why I've come to feel it's very important to do what's right, not just what's easy." Casey waited for him to go on, but Travis was silent.

"This thing is," she began tentatively, "if you really were connected with an important California hospital as my aunt suggested—"

"That's a closed chapter," Travis said, his mouth drawing into a tight line. Casey could see the dark anger in his eyes and decided to say no more on the subject.

Amanda Clark is the pseudonym for the mother-daughter writing team of Janet O'Daniel and Amy Midgley. They began collaborating on romances long-distance, when they lived in different states. Now they've both moved to South Carolina, which makes working together a lot less complicated. Janet and Amy have extensive writing backgrounds, including fiction, nonfiction and newspaper journalism. This is their third book for Harlequin Romance.

A NEIGHBORLY AFFAIR
Amanda Clark

Harlequin Books

TORONTO • NEW YORK • LONDON
AMSTERDAM • PARIS • SYDNEY • HAMBURG
STOCKHOLM • ATHENS • TOKYO • MILAN
MADRID • WARSAW • BUDAPEST • AUCKLAND

ISBN 0-373-03219-6

Harlequin Romance first edition September 1992

A NEIGHBORLY AFFAIR

CHAPTER ONE

THE FIRST DROPS of rain hit the windshield just as Casey spotted the sign—Barker Springs. Est. 1801. They trickled down the dusty glass, suddenly coming faster, and Casey turned on the wipers. But that only muddied the glass and made it even harder to see. She leaned forward tensely as she entered the town. Old trees lined the streets; big frame houses were set far back with green lawns in front of them. She could see slate sidewalks darkening from the rain, all of it dim and blurred through the track the wipers made. Then came a drugstore, a luncheonette, a supermarket and dry cleaner's. She kept driving, past the U.S. Post Office and Pete's Garage until she seemed to be nearly out of town again. On the right was a last building with a big painted sign in front: Elias Kelsey: Feed, Grain, Pet Supplies, Fertilizer.

Casey pulled into the parking lot where a scattering of other cars were parked, seized the *Washington Post* that lay on the seat beside her and unfolded it to make a covering for her head. She opened the car door and made a dash for the entrance marked Warehouse. She banged inside and found herself in a dim, grainy-smelling storeroom. Seated on bales, cartons and barrels were five men, all staring at her. A sixth man was standing with his back to her, pulling a heavy-looking bag from a pile and hoisting it onto his shoulder. One of the five seated men stood up and nodded in her direction.

"How do, ma'am. Something I can do for you?" He was lean and wiry and weathered-looking, and he smiled at her with flashing dentures.

"Oh—yes—that is, I'm looking for Mrs. Constance Pritchard's house." She had the distinct impression that this feed store, into which she'd just made a crashing entrance, was an all-male bastion and that she was interrupting what was probably a daily exchange of news and views. Several of the men were holding coffee mugs.

"Well, now. Do tell." He held out his hand and said, "I'm Elias Kelsey. This here's my place. Been here since 1928. Well, of course my father had it back then."

Casey put down her newspaper and shook the proffered hand. From behind Elias Kelsey she could see the man with the bag on his shoulder, who had turned toward her and was now watching with interest. He was younger than the others—in his thirties, she guessed— tall and blue-eyed, with a square jaw and a wide, mobile mouth that was curving into a faint smile.

"How do you do?" Casey asked a bit impatiently. "Is Mrs. Pritchard's place far from here? I really am anxious to find it..." She became aware, with a twinge of irritation, that the parking lot through which she'd just dashed had been muddy, and that her white sneakers and slacks were stained. Her pale turquoise silk blouse was spotted with rain.

"No, no. Not far at all," Elias Kelsey assured her. "What would you say, George? Two miles, maybe?"

"No more'n that, I don't believe," answered a man, speaking around the pipe clamped between his teeth.

"No, I'd say two miles, give or take a little," the proprietor said pleasantly.

"Fine," Casey said, trying to keep her impatience in check. "Could you please tell me how to get there? It's getting late and I'd like to..." Her voice trailed off as she glanced out the front window and saw the rain streaming down in torrents.

Elias Kelsey walked to the door. "What you want to do, you see," he said, pointing, "is turn your car around and go back the way you came. Go as far as the fork in the road and then bear right." He looked over his shoulder at the other men. "Route 116, Elwood? You live out that way."

"Well, yes, it's Route 116, only we always called it Lime Kill Road," said another man, sipping his coffee. "But I think the road sign came down a while back when they were doing some road work out that way. Bulldozer run right into the pole. Ed Marshall's boy was driving it—works for the county now, you know."

"That Ed's oldest boy?" another member of the group asked with sudden interest. "I thought he was in the service."

"Well, no, he's out now."

Casey looked incredulously from one to the other, then turned back to the proprietor. "So I should go about two miles out on that road?"

"I'd say about two miles, wouldn't you, Elwood? Out to Constance Pritchard's place?"

"Just about," Elwood agreed. "She's beyond the town line—you remember when they redrew the boundaries, don't you? Say, there was some fighting over that, I'll tell you."

A murmur of agreement swept through the group, and Casey's eyes caught on the face of the younger man with the bag still resting on one shoulder. He wore jeans and a plaid shirt and stood there in a relaxed yet undeniably confident stance. His smile reflected amusement as he watched the scene, taking in her impatience, as well as her spattered, rain-soaked appearance. He spoke for the first time.

"Two miles out—on your right. You can't miss it," he said. "Mailbox has her name on it."

"Thank you," Casey snapped, not appreciating his amused look.

"Guess you must be family," Elias Kelsey put in, and the expressions of the patrons became interested.

"Yes. Yes, I am. Thank you so much." Casey turned abruptly, unfolding her limp newspaper.

"That's a pretty hard rain out there," the younger man said as she started for the door.

"'Tis for a fact," Elias said. "Why not just sit for a spell till it lets up? We'll give you a cup of coffee."

"Thank you, but no," Casey tossed over her shoulder. "I really do have to be on my way." And she went dashing out the door into the rain. She was soaked through by the time she made it back to her car. She sat inside it for several moments, muttering to herself and, in her imagination, to her father, who had sent her on this errand.

"It's an old country place," he'd told her. "Upstate New York. Just get the property on the market and see that your aunt's getting proper medical care. Now that she's had this accident, it's the perfect time to make new arrangements for her. Your aunt Laura's anxious to have Constance move into her house in Short Hills."

"But you should be the one to do it!" Casey protested. "I don't even know her—well, hardly." Her aunt Constance had visited them only once, years before. Casey retained vague recollections of a flamboyant woman and remembered a general impression of uneasiness, as if no one had known quite what to say to her.

"Nonsense," Wright Logan had said, sounding every bit the senator. "You'll manage fine. Get in touch with some real estate people up there. It's good property— twenty-five acres. Do you good to take some responsibility. Besides, I've got that speech at the National Press Club, and after that I'll be meeting with my campaign committee pretty much on a daily basis."

Casey had felt her blood start to boil at such out-and-out manipulation, yet she'd never been able to stand up to her father. His forceful logic, indeed his very presence, had always caused her to back down. And her mother, pretty and shallow, had never been an ally. Angrily, Casey turned the ignition key and slammed the car into reverse. The car shot backward suddenly and there was a grinding crash of metal as she plowed into a huge tractor-trailer just pulling up to the loading platform of the feed store. She had neglected to snap on her seat belt, and the force of the collision sent her rebounding off the seat back and into the dashboard. She could feel the blow to her forehead and then an ominous warm trickle of blood.

Almost before she was aware of what had happened, someone was wrenching open the car door and dragging her out. She felt the pounding of the rain and then once again the grainy-sweet smell of the feed store as she was carried inside. Her silk shirt, spattered now with drops of blood, as well as rain, was clinging to her breasts, and her blond hair hung in wet wisps across her forehead.

"Got that first-aid kit handy, Elias?" Squinting up, Casey could see that it was the younger man, the one who'd looked at her in amusement. His face was serious now. "You'll be okay," he said quietly. "You just gave your head a whack. Everything else feel all right?" He placed her on a hay bale but still supported her with one arm. She found herself trembling. The arm at her back felt strong and capable.

"I don't know—I think so." She lifted a hand to the painful spot high on her forehead. She could see blood when she took it away.

"We'll clean that right off for you," he said reassuringly. "You're not seeing double or anything, are you?"

Casey swallowed and shook her head. "I'm fine," she said in something like her normal voice. "I'll just rest here for a minute, if you don't mind. Is my car..."

"We'll take a look as soon as we fix you up," he said, and Elias Kelsey came scurrying with a metal first-aid box.

"Cotton and disinfectant, I think that's probably all we need," the younger man said. "Maybe one of those bandages."

She felt the sting of the disinfectant as he applied it liberally with cotton. Then he stuck a small bandage over the spot.

"You're going to have a lump there," he said, "but the break in the skin isn't much. Still not feeling dizzy? No other pains?"

Casey shook her head again. "I'm perfectly all right," she insisted. "It's just a bump on the head. But I'd like to know about my car..."

George, the man with the pipe, came in, followed by the one called Elwood, both of them wearing raincoats. George shook his head sadly, although both men wore looks of suppressed excitement.

"You won't hardly be drivin' that car any time soon, Miss," George said.

Casey's heart sank, but then another alarming thought struck her. "Was anybody else hurt? The man in that truck?"

Elwood laughed, revealing some missing upper teeth. "Lord, I don't believe he even realizes anybody hit him. Truck that size don't feel much. You went right under that high bumper of his—little sporty car like yours, see—"

"Pretty well totaled the back end," George chimed in. "You're gonna need a tow truck to get it outta there."

Casey put both hands up to her face in sudden dismay. The tall man who had carried her in said, "Elias, you could call Pete's Garage, couldn't you? I'll drive the lady out to Constance Pritchard's place. I was going there, anyway. Let Pete collect her car and look it over, and when she's had a chance to recover she can talk to him about it."

"Sure thing, Travis," Elias Kelsey said. "We'll take care of it."

"I do appreciate that," Casey stammered. "I really do. Look, my name's Casey Logan, and please tell . . . Pete I'll take care of the towing expense and—"

Elias held up a hand. "Glad to do it for any kin of Constance's. You go along now, let Travis look after you."

Casey nodded weakly.

SETTLED INTO THE FRONT seat of a muddy Blazer, Casey dived into her roomy leather bag and checked her camera, which seemed to be intact and undamaged.

"Everything okay?" He finished stowing her suitcase in the back seat, along with the bag he'd hefted earlier, which turned out to be a fifty-pound bag of dog food.

"Yes. Thank you." She hadn't cared for the way he'd grinned at her before—a sort of mocking grin that told her he was sizing her up as an out-of-towner who probably couldn't find her way around a broom closet. Yet he'd been helpful—she owed him civility, at least. "I do appreciate your help, Mr. . .Travis, is it?"

"Travis Grant," he said, climbing into the driver's seat. "Are you a photographer?"

"Yes."

"Things or people?" He started the car and swung out of the feed store's parking lot. The rain was diminishing, and Casey kept her eyes resolutely away from the sight of her car, wedged pitifully under the huge truck. She had spoken briefly with the truck driver, a young man who had proven to be remarkably cheerful about the whole matter.

"What? Oh, well, both. Mostly people."

"For a paper? Magazine?"

"No—free-lance. I do portraits, parties, weddings, things like that."

"Weddings?" His eyebrows went up. "What are you doing up here in June, then? Why aren't you home taking care of business?"

Casey shot him a surprised look. "I just felt it was more important to come here and see about my aunt."

He seemed to consider this, then nodded. "Good thing you didn't have that suitcase in your trunk," he said, changing the subject abruptly. "Don't think I'd have been able to get it out."

She watched him as he guided the car along the wet road back through the town, humming softly under his breath. The hands holding the wheel were large and capable-looking, with long, square-tipped fingers. Casey found herself staring at them for a moment. Then surreptitiously she stole a look at his face. Seen in profile, it had a strong, craggy look. Dark hair, indifferently combed, fell forward; occasionally he reached up to push it back.

Casey felt something in her responding to him in an unfamiliar way, a way she disliked, since it seemed to indicate she wasn't in complete control. Hastily, to put such thoughts aside, she said, "I hope I'm not taking you far out of your way."

He didn't look at her. "No, that's where I was going anyway, to Constance's house."

"You were?" She frowned. "I thought you meant you were just going in this general direction."

"Nope." He jerked his head toward the back seat. "Promised her I'd pick up that dog food and drop it off."

Your aunt Constance is an animal lover, Casey's mother had told her with a pinched expression before she started out. *Be prepared.*

"How many dogs does she have?"

"It varies."

"Does she have horses, too?"

"Not at the moment. Were you planning on doing some riding while you're here?" Again she could hear the amusement in his voice.

"Not really. That is, not necessarily." Her head was starting to throb, and she felt a sense of confusion about exactly what she *had* been planning.

"Because your aunt's place may not be exactly what you're expecting."

"How do you know what I'm expecting?" she asked indignantly.

"Oh, I think I have a pretty good idea." He grinned, slanting her a look. "Old country home, faded but still stately. Traces of former elegance. Fences and barns, perhaps a horse or two. You figured on some country walks, a little riding and then home to—where is it, Washington? I noticed your newspaper—''

''I wasn't thinking anything of the sort,'' she snapped, annoyed at how close to the mark he'd come.

''Well, I only wondered, because you'll find it somewhat different.''

''None of that matters at all to me,'' she said coolly. ''I came because my aunt had an accident—a fall, I guess it was.''

''Yes. Off the porch roof.''

''How on earth did she do that?'' Casey asked, momentarily distracted.

''I'm not sure you'd believe me if I told you.'' He smiled again.

She looked at him, determined *not* to ask, since she suspected he was waiting for her to do so.

''And my father—we, my family—wanted to help out, that's all.''

''Great. I'm glad to hear it. She could use some help,'' he said simply. ''And here we are.''

He made a right turn into a dirt lane off the narrow blacktop road and parked the car. The rain had stopped, but the sky was still dark with clouds, and water dripped from all the trees. Casey peered out and caught her breath, staring at the house. It sprawled in every direction, as if its original structure had been added to over the years. One-story wings flanked the two-story center. The pillared front porch sagged perilously. The original paint, which must once have been white, had weathered to a mottled gray. Wet-looking chickens scratched in the front yard among old tires, kerosene cans, chains and discarded lumber. A yellow dog of uncertain ancestry dozed on the porch, and a cat slept on the roof of a rusty pickup truck.

This could not possibly be it, Casey thought, sitting in stunned silence. But Travis Grant was already opening his door and starting to unload the dog food.

"Go ahead," he said. "I'll be right with you. I'll put this in the kennel first. Don't worry about your suitcase. I'll bring it."

She watched him swing off toward the back where she saw several outbuildings. Once again he had the bag balanced on his shoulder. Casey opened the car door and got out gingerly, picking her way across the front yard and climbing the steps. The yellow dog looked up with interest as his tail wagged a welcome. She crossed the wavering boards of the porch to the front door and reached for the doorbell, but there were only twisted wires where it had once been. She raised a fist to knock, and at the same moment the door was wrenched open.

"Well! So you came, anyway. That man didn't listen to a word I said." The woman who stood there leaning on crutches was tall and solidly built. Long dark hair, heavily streaked with gray, flowed over her shoulders. She was wearing what appeared to be a series of garments donned in layers—a flowing skirt that reached her ankles, another shorter one over it, and a hip-length tunic over that, all in varying shades of blue and green. One foot was shod in a fuzzy pink slipper and the other was encased in a cast. Huge dark eyes glared angrily at Casey, and despite her surprise, Casey couldn't help thinking, *No wonder my father didn't want to come.* This was someone who wouldn't back down easily, even to Wright Logan.

"Aunt Constance?" she said. "I'm Casey Logan. We met a long time ago when you visited us, and you probably don't remember me, but—"

"I've tried my best to put all memory of that visit out of my mind," the woman said in a loud husky voice. "Mercifully, I've succeeded quite well. What in the world have you done to yourself?" She glanced from the bandage down to the soaked and muddy sneakers.

"It's nothing—a little trouble with my car. Aunt Constance, I know my father's spoken with you by telephone," Casey floundered on. "He thought it might be helpful if I—"

"My brother's used to managing people," the woman interrupted, her lip curling slightly. She showed no sign of inviting Casey over the threshold. "However, I don't care to be managed. And since I can only assume that's what you're here for, I'm sorry you had a long trip for nothing. I'll tell you what I told him. I'm not selling my property, and I'm not moving in with my sister Laura and that gray pinstripe husband of hers just to suit my brother and get myself off his conscience. Forget it. This is my home and this is where I'm staying." She looked past Casey. "Isn't that Travis Grant's car?"

Seconds later, he rounded the house and waved at her. "Hi, Constance. I just put the dog food in the kennel."

Constance Pritchard's eyes went from one to the other. "You two have met?"

"Just about half an hour ago," he said cheerfully, taking the porch steps two at a time. "Well, what are we standing out here for?"

"I haven't been invited in," Casey said coldly.

His eyebrows shot up and he turned to the woman in the doorway, giving her a reproachful look. "Constance, are you being ungracious again?"

The woman's gaze shifted uncomfortably, and she moved back with some reluctance. "Oh, all right. We might as well go in, I suppose." She limped into the house on her crutches and Casey and Travis Grant followed. "Except I already know why she's here," Constance muttered. "She wants to sell the place out from under me and pack me off to my sister Laura's. Laura lives in Short Hills, New Jersey, and her husband's a banker."

Casey bit her tongue to keep from retorting that it sounded like a major step up from this place. They walked into a large front hall and then through an archway into what must have been a living room originally, but now seemed to be a catchall place, a kind of command post from which the injured Constance Pritchard could operate. A large recliner chair stood squarely in the middle of the room, surrounded by books, magazines, boxes of tissues, thermos bottles, reading glasses. On the floor beside the chair was a cardboard carton cut down on one side for easy entry. The yellow dog, who had come in with them, now curled up on the old bath towel that lined it. The room was high-ceilinged and must once have displayed a certain elegance, Casey thought, observing its carved moldings and fireplace detail. Constance sank into the recliner, her injured leg stretched out in front of her.

"Where'd you get a name like Casey?" she demanded.

"It's a nickname really. My name's Katharine Case Logan, you see, and in school they started calling me K.C."

"That's right. Your mother was a Case. Well, in more ways than one," Constance said, grinning at her own joke. "How is Felicia, anyway?"

"Fine." Casey sat on a rump-sprung chair near the fireplace. Travis Grant squatted down beside Constance, lifted her long skirt and ran his hands over her cast. "Is this bothering you, Constance?"

"Not any more than a skunk in the parlor," she snapped. "Of course it's bothering me. And when do I get rid of these things?" She motioned toward the crutches she'd tossed down beside her chair.

"Pretty soon. When that leg's strong enough to stand some weight I'll get you one of those canes with the feet."

Casey stared first at Constance, then at Travis. "Are you a *doctor?*" she asked incredulously.

"Certainly he's a doctor," Constance said. "I thought you two had already met."

"Well, we did, but..." Casey remembered the strong, skillful hands swabbing her forehead, applying the bandage. She remembered the questions—*double vision? Anything else hurt?* But how could she have been expected to know? Anyone might ask such questions. "I see," she said.

"Your niece had an accident herself," Travis Grant said.

"I thought she looked a little dragged out," Constance said. "What happened to her?" They spoke as if Casey wasn't present.

"It was raining pretty hard, and she backed into a truck down at Elias Kelsey's feed store. Got quite a bump on her head."

Ready for scorn from this unwelcoming woman, Casey was surprised to see her nodding in an understanding way. "Easy to do that," she said calmly. "Cars have a way of going where they want to. I never trust machines. Lucky it wasn't any worse."

"Mr.—Dr. Grant says you were hurt in a fall off the porch roof," Casey said. "How did that happen, Aunt Constance?"

The woman gave a nonchalant wave of one hand. "Oh, I'd climbed up there to rescue Walter and lost my footing."

Casey nodded. Walter. A cat? The yellow dog? She skipped over the possibilities. Constance supplied the answer.

"Beaver," she said. "He's around here somewhere. He can't resist an open window, but once he got out there he froze and wouldn't budge."

"I see," Casey answered weakly. "And you have other pets, as well?"

Dark eyes glared at her. "I don't care for that word *pets*. It's demeaning. They're beings, the same as we are. Fellow sojourners on the planet."

"Yes, of course." Casey glanced quickly at Travis Grant and found wry amusement in his blue eyes.

"Your niece says she's come to help you out," he said. "That should be great for you—having somebody stay with you till you're back on your feet."

Casey shot him a startled look. His assumption that she was moving in on a long-term basis sounded alarming. Besides, Constance Pritchard had given no indication so far that her niece was welcome, even overnight.

"A motel will do perfectly well for me," Casey said hastily, more than a little annoyed that he was being so presumptuous and speaking for her.

"Oh, but then you wouldn't be much help to your aunt, would you?" he said. "And that's what you want to do, isn't it—help out?"

His words mocked her, and so did the raised eyebrows, the quizzical look.

"It seems to me she could do with some help," Casey said, glancing around the cluttered room.

Constance, fidgeting uncomfortably in the big recliner, made a quick brushing-away motion with one hand. "Oh, well, I suppose she could stay for a night or two. But as far as that help business is concerned, I'm *not* going to be helped out of my house."

"No, of course you're not," Travis Grant reassured her.

Bursting with suppressed anger, Casey glared at him.

"You're done with office hours, aren't you?" Constance asked the doctor. "Stay and have some supper with us, why don't you? As long as she's going to be here, anyway..." She jerked her head in Casey's direction.

He must have heard Casey's sharp intake of breath, but if he did, he only smiled. "Great idea, Constance. Only you sit here—the two of us can fix things. Right, Miss Logan?"

"Casey," she heard herself saying. "My name's Casey."

"If you call that a name," Constance snorted.

CHAPTER TWO

WHILE THE DOCTOR went out to his car for her suitcase, Casey followed her aunt's directions to the kitchen. It was a big room in the back of the house with a huge wooden table at its center. An ancient gas range—as large as a limousine, she thought—occupied one wall, its low oven door held closed by a stick propped at an angle on the floor. Every counter was covered with pots and pans, cereal boxes, bottled salad oil, cans of tuna, packages of rice, noodles, coffee, tea bags. On the table lay a plastic red-and-white-checked tablecloth. An old-fashioned cut-glass tumbler in the middle held a bunch of spoons.

Casey stared around in consternation. The small amount of cooking she'd done had been in efficient, modern surroundings and had relied heavily on a microwave oven. Where did one start in a place like this? She heard a crashing and banging overhead, then footsteps descending, and Travis Grant appeared in the doorway.

"The spare bedroom's the one to the left at the top of the stairs," he said brusquely. "The window showed some reluctance to open, that's what the noise was. I thought the room ought to be aired out a little."

His words had an ominous sound of cobwebs and mustiness, Casey thought.

"My aunt said something about a chicken," she said uncertainly.

"Oh, sure." He strode over to the refrigerator and brought it out. Casey stared at the chicken as he put it on the counter by the sink. "We can broil it," he said.

"It's all in one piece," Casey said in a doubtful voice.

He shot her a contemptuous look. "Forgot you were a city girl. You're used to those little packages wrapped in plastic with all the pieces separate."

She started to answer back, but he went on talking as he reached for a knife and began cutting the chicken up with quick skillful strokes. "How are you on boiling eggs?"

"I'm sure I can manage," Casey said through gritted teeth.

"And I saw lettuce in a plastic bag in there," he continued, obviously unperturbed. "Michael must have picked it this morning. You could see if it's been washed."

In the cool silence that followed, she set about finding the things he'd mentioned. At last she asked, "Who's Michael? Someone who works here?"

"Kid from across the road. Lives there with his mother, Shirley. Shirley works at the hospital in Addison Mills—that's twenty miles north of here, but she helps Constance out a lot."

"This looks clean to me," Casey said, peering into the plastic bag full of crisp green leaf lettuce.

"I guess Shirley washed it."

"It must be hard for my aunt to have to hire people. She's obviously not too well fixed for money."

He glanced up from the chicken he was arranging for the broiler. "Shirley doesn't take any money," he said coldly. "She's just a good neighbor. Constance insists on paying Michael a little for looking after the kennel, feeding the animals and so on, but it's not much.''

"Oh.'' She felt momentarily embarrassed. Then she asked, "What's this kennel business? Does she raise dogs?''

"No, she just takes them in. Strays. That sort of thing. And cats, too. Anything that comes along.''

"Isn't there an SPCA around here?'' Casey ran water over the eggs and carried them to the stove.

"You'll need a match,'' he said.

She found them on the counter, struck one and turned on the gas. It whooshed loudly, then lighted.

"There's an SPCA up beyond Addison Mills, but that's pretty far, and besides, they've got their hands full. Constance just does what she can around here.''

"That costs money, too,'' she said severely.

"Well, that's up to her, isn't it?'' He shrugged with a nonchalance that infuriated Casey.

"Up to a point, yes. But now she's been hurt, and she's having a hard time managing. For heaven's sake, just look around.'' Casey took in the cluttered kitchen with a glance. "This place'll be doing well just to make it through another winter. The first major crisis—heating, electrical—could wipe her out financially. If not worse.'' With a shudder, Casey thought of fires and bursting pipes.

"She's only going to be in that cast another few weeks, you know. And before her accident she was energetic, completely capable.''

"Aunt Laura and Uncle Ed have a beautiful house with plenty of room for Constance.''

"Where she'd be completely miserable.''

"And with people to look after her. The family only wants what's best for her.''

"How can you know what's best for someone you just met a half hour ago?" He removed the stick from the oven door and slid the chicken inside. There was another whoosh as he lit the broiler with a match.

"I've met her before," Casey muttered. "And after all, we are family. It's very obvious to me that she'd be much better off selling her property. My father thinks—"

"Ah yes. The great Senator Logan thinks. Well, why doesn't the senator help her out if he's so concerned?"

Casey felt herself reddening. "He has every intention of doing just that," she said indignantly. "That's what I'm here for. Once these business details are cleared up, he'll certainly help her with anything she may need."

"I see." His blue eyes raked her with a sardonic look. "But not a cent to keep her in a place where she's happy."

"Look here," Casey said, making no effort to control her anger, "this is really none of your business, Dr. Grant."

"Oh, make it Travis, why don't you? We're getting along so well," he said, slamming the oven door shut and propping it into place with the stick again.

They went on with their preparations, but in silence now. There was a momentary flurry when Constance came limping into the kitchen later. Casey had set the table, and in spite of herself she could feel some of her angry mood dissipating as she looked at the crisp French bread, the black olives, the hard-cooked eggs, garden-fresh greens and the golden chicken, savory smelling with rosemary and thyme.

Constance settled herself at the table, dropping her crutches to the floor and inhaling deeply.

"That *does* smell good," she said. "How do you like being invited to a meal you have to cook yourself, Travis?" She gave his arm a poke.

"It was a joint effort," he said curtly.

They were just sitting down when there was a knock at the screen door. A boy of sixteen or so was standing there. Casey could see brown hair, thick and mussed, T-shirt and jeans.

"Hi, Mrs. Pritchard," he said. "Anything else you need? They've all been fed and watered. Everything looks okay. Hi, Dr. Grant."

"Hi, Mike. I guess everything's okay here," Travis answered. "Will you be coming to mow my lawn on Saturday?"

"You bet. I didn't forget."

"This is Miss Logan," Travis said. "She's come to visit for a while. Michael Townsend."

"Hi," the boy replied, bobbing his head politely.

"Hello, Mike."

"Take some lettuce home to your mother," Constance ordered. "See you tomorrow, Michael."

The sun had come out and was streaming in through the screen door and the window over the sink, casting shadows and turning ordinary objects to soft gold. There was a sudden harsh screech outside followed by several more like it. Casey looked around, startled.

"Blue jays dive-bombing the cat," Constance said calmly.

Casey nodded. As they filled their plates and started eating, she felt more hungry than she would have imagined. The broiled chicken with its delicate herb seasoning was delicious, the bread crisp and fresh.

"Is the beaver, er, Walter, tame enough to be around the house?" she asked after a moment.

"Oh, yes. He's here somewhere." Constance waved a chicken leg. "He usually tags after Michael. You'll be seeing him, don't worry."

"How do you happen to have him?"

Constance stared at her as if the answer should be perfectly obvious. "He needed a home."

"He was caught in a trap when he was just a kit," Travis Grant explained. "He's still a little gimpy."

"But shouldn't he go back to the water now—or wherever he came from?"

"Should," Constance agreed. "Except that his family wouldn't want him anymore. He'd be an outsider, and beavers are real huffy about outsiders. I don't think he'd make it."

"He'd be too apt to trust people, for one thing, and then he'd be sure to get hurt," Travis added.

Even so, Casey thought to herself, Walter had been the cause of Constance's fall, and the dogs whose distant barking and yipping she could hear through the screen door were probably eating her out of house and home. Remembering her father's orders, she tried to bring the conversation back to practical matters.

"About your leg, Aunt Constance," she began tentatively. "Daddy was anxious for me to send the X rays to him so that he could pass them along to an orthopedic man he knows in New York."

She saw a faint flush of color rise in Travis Grant's face, but he went on eating and did not look at her.

"He's worried about that, too?" Constance asked with irritation. "Good grief, why didn't he come himself? Well no, that wouldn't be any good, would it? I'm not the right image for Senator Logan's reelection campaign."

Casey ignored the thrust, uneasily aware that it might be close to the truth. "It's just that he wants you to get the best possible care," she said, trying to sound reasonable.

"Honestly, I don't know what my brother's thinking of. I'm getting the best possible care right here. Travis used to be on the staff of one of the finest hospitals in California."

Casey darted a quick look of surprise at him. "That may be, of course," she said. "I'm not saying anything against the quality of Dr. Grant's treatment, Aunt Constance. But he isn't at that hospital now, is he? And medical resources here must be very limited—"

"It's perfectly all right," Travis interrupted. "I'd be happy for you to have the X rays. My office is in town. If you'd like to stop by, you can pick them up any time." He changed the subject quickly, as if with a deliberate effort. "Washington's your home, is it?"

Flustered, Casey answered, "Yes. Dad rents a house there, since he's in Washington so much. Home's New York, actually, and he and Mother spend a lot of time there, but I stay on in Washington even when they're gone."

"Your niece is a photographer, Constance. Did you know that?"

Constance's dark, expressive eyebrows went up. "You don't say." For a moment her glance lingered on Casey in an appraising way as if she still hadn't made a full assessment of her. Then she asked, much as Travis had, "What do you photograph?"

"Things. And people," Casey answered lightly. "For example, I'd like to photograph you, Aunt Constance."

Now it was Constance whose cheeks showed a slight touch of color. Yet Casey had not said it to flatter her;

quite simply, she was fascinated by the play of light and shadow on her aunt's strong features, by the way her hair sprang back from her broad forehead. Seated at the table in the old kitchen, with the breeze blowing the thin curtain at the open window behind her, she might have been the subject of a Wyeth painting.

"Well. My goodness." Constance spoke decisively, as if to put an end to the subject, and reached for another of the moist black olives. Yet the blush of pink remained in her cheeks, Casey noticed.

Later she and Travis did the dishes in near-total silence while Constance limped back to her chair in the living room and opened her newspaper. Distantly they could hear her occasional comments, made to the room at large. "Highway Department complaining about an inadequate budget again. Ha! Suppose that's why they can't get around to fixing that pothole in front of my house... Still haven't got that roof on the Methodist church, I see..."

Plunging her hands into the hot soapy water, Casey said at last, "I hope you don't think I meant to imply you weren't giving my aunt adequate care. It's just that—"

"Oh, I understand." Drying a tall iced-tea glass, he slanted a wry, half-amused look at her. "You just don't think a hick doctor who drives a car like mine could possibly handle a fractured leg, even a fairly routine one."

Casey felt flustered. "No, it's not that at all. But my father especially urged that I send him those X rays. He's anxious for her to have the very best of care. Oh, dear, I don't mean it to sound— The thing is, it's very hard to argue with my father. He's a man used to giving orders, arranging things. Not that he's overbearing, I don't mean that..."

"I suppose he's someone used to power. I've had a little experience with that—being up against power. That's why I've come to feel that it's very important to do what's right, not just what's easy." Casey waited for him to go on, but he was silent, as if he'd already said more than he intended.

She thrust the silverware into the water and began washing it. "The thing is, if you really were connected with an important California hospital as my aunt suggested..."

"That's a closed chapter," he said, his mouth drawing into a tight line. Casey, glancing at him, could see the dark anger in his eyes and decided to say no more on the subject. They finished the dishes in silence.

"Can I help you upstairs, Constance?" he asked when they rejoined her.

"I wouldn't mind," she admitted. "Beats going up one step at a time on my rear end. Besides, how often do I get that close to a good-looking man?"

He grinned and swung her easily into his arms. Casey followed, carrying the crutches, and as she watched the tall figure mount the stairs, Constance's arm around his neck and the blue and green skirts flowing around them both, she felt an odd tremor of excitement at his strength, at the effortless way he carried the older woman. What must it feel like, she wondered, to be enclosed in those arms, tenderly cared for, with the whole world outside, shut away? Casey swallowed and gave herself a small shake, following briskly as he led the way into Constance's bedroom. She placed the crutches within easy reach of the bed, an old-fashioned brass affair that stood amid the same sort of clutter as the chair in the living room. Books, a small bedside radio, reading lamp. The rug was flowered, worn down to the webbing in many places. From outside the open window came a scent of roses.

"Thanks, Travis," Constance said. "I can manage fine now." She glanced at Casey. "You can stay up a while if you want to, girl. Just lock the front door and turn the lights out when you come up."

Casey wondered how long it would be before Constance called her by name. "I will. Let me know if you need anything, Aunt Constance."

As she and Travis went back downstairs, he said, "I'd better be going. I have a couple of house calls to make yet."

"House calls! I thought those were a thing of the past."

"Not in Barker Springs. We practice a different kind of medicine here."

His cool tone made the comment a subtle dig, but Casey decided not to react to it. "Thanks for your help," she said. "You know, the ride out here, the chicken and drying the dishes and all that."

"My pleasure." And then, before she could say any more, he had pushed open the front screen door and was gone. Casey was almost sorry that he'd left so abruptly, yet relieved, after the disturbing jumble of emotions she had felt earlier.

The yellow dog, whose name she hadn't learned, had come up behind her and was nosing at the door. "Is this your time to go out, boy?" she asked, opening it for him and stepping onto the front porch.

The June evening was mild and fragrant with the scent of a huge climbing rosebush with scarlet blooms that overhung the porch. Another with white blossoms climbed a trellis at the far end. Casey sank into an old rocking chair and began to rock slowly in the last of the thickening twilight. How much more complicated it all was than she'd anticipated! It had sounded so reasonable when her father described the situation and told her in that forceful way of his to drive up and straighten it all out for him. "Just put the property on the market and explain to your aunt how much better off she'd be at Laura's." But Constance Pritchard was a strong, independent woman who wanted to stay in her own house. And it was easy to see why she resented Casey for suggesting she do otherwise.

Casey watched the old yellow dog trotting briskly off toward the back of the house. From the kennel she heard one faint yip and then silence. Still, despite Constance's feelings, the reality was all around her—signs of neglect everywhere, of not enough money to keep the place up. Peeling paint and ancient plumbing. A disaster waiting to happen. So her father was not entirely wrong, was he? And Constance *was* sublimely impractical, eating through what few resources she did have, throwing them away on this white elephant of a house, on the stray animals who were certainly consuming every extra dollar. Only now that she'd seen her again, Casey had to admit she couldn't picture Constance in her Aunt Laura's sleek suburban home, surrounded by deep-pile rugs and soft thick towels with centers that weren't worn through.

Sighing, Casey reached up and rubbed her forehead, her hand touching the bandage and feeling the sudden tenderness there. At once her heart started an unaccountable pounding as she remembered Travis Grant bending over her. *You just gave your head a whack. Everything else feel all right?*

No, Casey thought soberly, rocking back and forth. Nothing felt right. Nothing was the way it should be, nothing the way she'd anticipated. And how was she ever going to sort it all out? For several minutes she sat there rocking. Finally she got up, whistled softly for the dog, and when he came trotting back, went into the house with him, locking the door behind her.

The bed in her room was iron and painted white. The carpet had big cabbage roses scattered over it, and was only slightly less worn than Constance's. Thin white curtains blew in at the open window. A light in the ceiling turned on with a dangling string.

Casey unpacked her suitcase, hurried across the hall to the old-fashioned bathroom and returned to slide between the sheets. She shifted around to find a smooth spot between lumps in the thin mattress. She could hear night sounds from outside—soft rustlings, movements, murmurs, the activity of whatever creatures came to life after dark. A tree branch scraped softly against the screen. Once a car drove by, and she wondered if it might be Travis Grant, returning from his house calls. All was quiet down the hall, where her aunt's room was. The soft darkness closed around her and her eyes drifted shut.

A small, squeaking sound caused them to fly open as she heard the door to her room being pushed ajar. She'd noticed earlier that the latch fitted improperly. Casey held her breath. "Who is it?" she whispered.

There was no answer other than a small, shuffling sound, and then something heaved itself up onto the bed, panting, and struggling. Casey caught a whiff of damp, mossy odor and in the moonlight saw the bulky outline of a creature dragging something behind it. Like a shot she leapt out of bed. If that was a cat who'd brought some dead thing into the house . . . She grabbed for the overhead light string and pulled.

Startled and squinting, the fat beaver stared at her, his long front teeth gleaming. His flat, muscular tail trailed after him. As she stared helplessly back, he sat on his hind legs, small front paws dangling. Casey was torn between annoyance and the desire to laugh.

"Walter?" she asked tentatively.

The beaver seemed to take that as a welcome and settled himself comfortably at the foot of the bed. Casey stood there for a moment watching him, then tiptoed across the room to her bag and reached inside for her camera.

CHAPTER THREE

EVERY MUSCLE in her body hurt when Casey got up the next morning, and she concluded that a car accident, even a minor one, produced stresses that weren't immediately apparent. She tried to stretch, but found it too painful, and settled for a hot bath in the claw-footed tub across the hall. She felt somewhat better after drying herself and slipping into jeans and a T-shirt.

She decided her first errand should be a trip into the village to find out about repairs to her car and to locate a real-estate agent. Her aunt might not be convinced that selling her property was the wisest course, but a discussion of prices and some reasonable arguments about how her situation could be improved might influence her, Casey thought. She brushed her shoulder-length blond hair and twisted it into a single thick braid. Then, standing at the old-fashioned mirror in her room, she applied lipstick lightly. She had removed the bandage from her forehead and was relieved to see only a small cut. The area surrounding it was discoloring in a fairly spectacular way, but that would pass.

The question now was how to get into town. Her aching muscles were already resisting the thought of a two-mile hike. Turning away from the mirror, she looked out the window toward the rusted pickup where the cat was once again napping, this time on the hood.

After breakfast she asked Constance about it.

"Does that thing run?" They stood on the front porch regarding the truck.

"Did the last time I tried it," Constance said. "Of course I haven't been in it since my accident. And the battery *did* seem a little weak..." She gave an offhand shrug. She was wearing another of her voluminous layered outfits, with the addition, this morning, of a red shawl knotted around her shoulders. "You could give it a try."

The old truck's engine did indeed fail to turn over. The cat opened one eye and continued to sleep on the hood. "It's the battery, all right. You probably need a new one," Casey informed her aunt. "I'll talk to the garage man about that, too."

"No hurry," Constance said. "I'm not going anywhere."

Casey suppressed a groan. She was used to the efficiency of a household with Wright Logan at the head of it, where fresh paint and live batteries were considered standard, where clean dishes were put away in cupboards rather than left on the counter and where dandelions were ruthlessly routed from the lawn, not left to flourish in lavish profusion.

"But how am I going to get into town?" she asked as she rejoined Constance on the porch.

"I have a bicycle," Constance said thoughtfully.

By the time she'd pedaled into Barker Springs, Casey ached all over and was beginning to think walking would have been easier. She went at once to Pete's Garage to inquire about her car. Pete proved to be a big burly man with a ready smile and grease-stained hands, who led her around her car, pointing and explaining.

"Sure, me and my son can do it," he said. He jerked his head in the direction of a younger man built like him, who was buffing a newly painted fender on another car. "He's good on body work. Looks to me as if we may have to order you a new bumper, though. Gas tank, too."

"How long will it take?" Casey asked, gazing with sorrow at her neat little sports car, its back end twisted and smashed.

"Oh—week or ten days, I s'pose. You might want to get some pictures of it for your insurance company."

"I'll take them myself," Casey said, pulling out her camera. A week or ten days was longer than she'd been planning to stay, but there seemed to be no alternative. In any case, as things stood now, it might well take longer than that to bring her aunt around to an acceptance of the realities. She photographed the car from several angles, then explained about the old truck and the battery that was needed. Pete agreed to take care of it. "I'll run out that way this afternoon," he said.

"Could you tell me who's a reputable real-estate agent here?" she asked as she was leaving.

He looked at her curiously. "Ain't but one, really," he said. "Lee Nelson. You'll see the office next door to the drugstore."

Casey thanked him and paid in advance for the battery he was to deliver and install. Then she pedaled off down the street, stopping at the drugstore for rubber gloves and a bottle of shampoo. As she came out, she glanced into the real-estate office, where she could see a receptionist sitting at a desk. She hesitated for a moment, but cycled past it until she reached a big, white corner house she'd noticed on the way into town. A shingle hung from a lamp pole in front: Travis Grant, M.D. The house had a broad veranda that went around two sides and old-fashioned double-hung windows that reached the floor. Casey stared at it for several moments, then wheeled her bicycle up the walk and left it leaning against the front railing as she mounted the steps and rang the bell.

Footsteps sounded from the other side of the door, and it was opened by a woman in a large denim apron. She was tall and gray-haired and had a strong, wiry look.

"Good morning." Casey hesitated.

"Good morning. Did you want to see the doctor? He's at the hospital this morning, but he'll have office hours this afternoon at two."

"No, no. I don't need to see him. I was just stopping by for some X rays he said I could have."

"Oh, yes. You must be Miss Logan." The woman gave her a friendly smile. "They're here on the hall table. I'm Anna Bates. I do a little housekeeping for the doctor. Come in, won't you, Miss Logan?" She opened the door wide, and Casey paused only a second before stepping inside.

It was a cool, dim, high-ceilinged hallway, with arches to the right and left. The one on the right seemed to open into a waiting room—Casey saw a table with well-thumbed magazines and in the corner a box of toys. To the left of the hall was a living room, sparsely furnished but pleasant. The couch, chairs and tables had a random look, as though they might have been picked out at different times and places.

"I was just about to make myself a sandwich and a cup of tea," Anna Bates said socially. "Come and have something with me, why don't you?"

Casey studied her with some surprise, wondering if all strangers were invited in so readily. "Oh, thank you, but really, I couldn't. I wouldn't want to—"

"It wouldn't put me out at all, if that's what you mean," the woman said, already starting toward the back of the house. "I'd enjoy the company. You're Constance Pritchard's niece, isn't that what the doctor said?"

"I am, yes." Casey paused uncertainly, then followed her. "I've come to try and help out my aunt a little if I can. My father's been concerned about her since her accident."

"Well, isn't that grand. Constance must be just tickled to have you."

"Tickled" wasn't exactly the word, Casey thought. They reached the kitchen, a huge room, scrubbed and orderly, and with the same kind of big round table as Constance's. Everything looked efficient and well cared for, yet comfortable. She could smell the delicious aroma of fresh baking; there was a loaf of bread on a wooden cutting board in the middle of the table, and beside it a baked ham.

"I shouldn't be cutting this bread," Anna Bates fussed, motioning Casey to a chair. "It's hardly had a chance to cool through properly. Oh, well..." She picked up a bread knife and cut several thick slices. "I made an extra loaf—you could take it to Constance. She loves my oatmeal bread."

"It looks wonderful." Casey sat gingerly at the table and watched as the housekeeper turned to the ham and began working on it. "I really don't like you to go to all this trouble, though."

Anna Bates waved the large carving knife, dismissing her protest. "Don't you love that place of your aunt's, though?" She grinned, slapping ham lavishly on the fresh bread. "We all do. Of course, she's had a hard time keeping it up by herself since her husband died and even more since her accident, but it's still a real treasure. And that barn of hers!''

''I haven't seen that yet.''

''Oh, Lordy, the things she's got in there! She just can't throw anything away. But she'll give it away. That's something else again. Why, when Dr. Grant came to Barker Springs three years ago he didn't have a stick of furniture or even a towel. Most of that stuff in the living room she gave him. He'd just got here from California then, and it was after the wedding— Well, of course, there never actually *was* a wedding.'' She left this statement dangling tentatively as she shoved the sandwich toward Casey and poured her a cup of tea from a big brown pot.

''Right about that time Constance's husband took sick and the doctor cared for him. They got to be good friends before Frank died—wasn't anything the doctor could do to save him, but he was a great comfort to both of 'em, even so. Constance always said that.''

Casey nodded and took a bite of the sandwich. Fresh-baked bread and country-style ham mingled succulently. Why was she so much hungrier here than at home?

''Guess you were lucky he was there at the club yesterday when you arrived,'' Anna said, sitting down with her own sandwich.

''The club?''

''That's what I call Elias Kelsey's feed store. Didn't you see all the regulars there? They hang around and swap stories. The doctor says he doesn't know what's going on in town unless he stops in there every day or so.''

Casey smiled, thinking she'd guessed right about the place. She was about to ask more questions when the back door opened and Travis Grant came in. He was dressed much as he'd been the day before, except that today he was wearing a blue knit shirt with his jeans. His eyes seemed to pick up the color and looked even bluer than Casey remembered. His glance moved between the two women. "Well. Good morning," he said. He wasn't smiling, but it seemed to Casey that some of the bristling resentment she'd noticed the day before was missing.

"I was just in town to see about my car," Casey said hurriedly, feeling a need to explain her presence. "When I stopped here Mrs. Bates kindly invited me to have some lunch with her."

"Not easy to say no to Anna," he commented dryly. He said nothing about the X rays. "How'd you get here?"

"Aunt Constance's bicycle."

He whistled. "How'd that feel? You had a few sore muscles this morning, I'll bet."

"A few," she admitted. He seemed to fill up the big kitchen, charging the air with an odd tension, a kind of electricity.

"You had some calls," Anna said, getting up and going to the counter for a slip of paper. "Roger Borden's mother said his cough sounds funny and could she bring him in this afternoon. Myra Byrne's coming with her husband at two, if that's all right. Oh, and Dr. Leland Somers called again."

Travis, who had slid into a chair at the table with them, looked up quickly. "Dr. Somers?"

"Yes. He wanted to know if you'd thought any more about what you and he discussed. He sounded kind of anxious."

Travis ran a hand through his hair. Casey, watching him without understanding, felt a pull of emotions in him. Something was troubling him; she sensed it might be a decision he had to make and was putting off.

"I'll call him back," Travis said.

Anna Bates's eyes darted between the two of them. "Goodness, I forgot to cut roses this morning," she said, fishing into the pocket of her denim apron for a pair of clippers. "Better do it before they open up too much."

"Aren't you going to finish your lunch?" Travis demanded.

"Haven't started it yet. You eat that sandwich—I'll make myself another later." She glanced quickly from him to Casey again, then left by the back door.

"I feel terribly in the way," Casey said. "I'm sure you're busy."

He pulled the sandwich toward him and poured himself a cup of tea. "You're a patient, too, after all," he said matter-of-factly, and before Casey could speak again, he reached over to lift the hair gently off her forehead, examining the cut. "Looks pretty good, even if the first aid did come from a hick doctor."

The light touch of his fingers made Casey shiver inside, and for the first time she saw a faint glimmer of amusement in his face. "I suppose I should apologize," she began. "I know you must be holding it against me, what I said about the X rays. I didn't mean to be critical. It's just that my father thought—"

"Ah, yes. The senator again." Before she could answer, he changed the subject. "What about your car? Did you talk to Pete?"

She nodded and told him about the necessary repairs. They made polite conversation for several minutes, sticking to the subject of the damaged car while they finished their sandwiches. By then Anna Bates was back in the house with a handful of creamy roses.

"I'm going to send some of these to Constance," Anna said. "I know she's got beautiful roses of her own, but you can't have too many. Now don't forget to take the bread when you go."

"And the X rays," Travis said pointedly, getting up from the table. He gave Casey a long look.

"Thank you," she mumbled.

He excused himself and headed for the front of the house, where Casey presumed his office was located. Moments later she, too, got up to leave, thanking the housekeeper and trying to remember all the messages she was to give Constance.

"Please don't bother," she said as Anna Bates started to put down her clippers and dry her hands. The table was now scattered with roses ready to be arranged in jugs and vases. "I can find my way out."

"All right," the woman said cheerfully. "Tell Constance I'll see her Friday."

"All right. And thanks again." Casey edged out of the kitchen, her arms full of roses and fresh bread. She glanced into the waiting room before opening the front door, but it was still empty and quiet. As she passed the hall table where the brown envelope containing the X rays lay, she paused for a second, but went out without picking it up. Outside, she stowed her burdens in the bicycle's basket, climbed on and pedaled briskly toward the fork in the road, along the route that was already becoming familiar. Thoughts and impressions were spinning around in her head, words spoken and not understood. *Well, of course there never actually was a wedding...* What kind of troubled past had Travis Grant left behind him in California? And, Casey wondered, was it any of her business, anyway?

MICHAEL TOWNSEND, her aunt's kennel helper, was at the side of the house bathing a dog when she returned. He'd set up an old-fashioned zinc tub in the bright June sunshine. A small black dog, well lathered, shivered unhappily and looked up at the boy, liquid eyes voicing a silent protest.

"Hello!" Casey slipped off the bike, leaning it against the clapboard wall, then walked over to watch.

"Hi." The teenager gave her a shy smile and went back to his work.

"I thought you'd be in school."

"Today was the last day. We got out early."

"He doesn't seem to be enjoying that much," Casey observed, squatting down beside the tub.

"You got that right," Michael said. "And he has to be bathed three times a week."

"Why so often?" Casey was reaching into her large shoulder bag for her camera.

Michael went on with his lathering. "He was a stray, see. Mrs. Pritchard found him out in the ditch there. He was real tiny."

"He's not very big now."

"No. But the thing is, he had everything wrong with him. He couldn't walk hardly, and the vet said he had rickets, mange, malnutrition, dehydration—a whole lot of stuff. These baths are for the mange, mostly. He has to take vitamins and medicine, too."

Sizable veterinarian's bills loomed up in Casey's mind.

"I suppose my aunt tries to find homes for as many of the animals as she can." He nodded. "It doesn't seem as if anybody would want to adopt a pet who's got so much wrong with him," she suggested.

"No, maybe not." Michael shrugged. "We might just wind up keeping him here. He'll probably turn out to be a real good dog someday."

There was something touching about such youthful optimism. Casey adjusted her lens opening and held up the camera.

"You don't mind if I take a few pictures, do you?" she asked. "It might be fun to remember him the way he looks now, all soapy."

"Sure, go ahead," Michael said agreeably.

It was a made-to-order composition, Casey thought. Boy and dog, with the old house and its scarlet rosebush in the background. The little dog turned his head to follow her movements, as she circled the tub, shooting picture after picture. A cap of white suds covered his floppy ears. The soft eyes sought her out. Michael bent over him, his tousled hair catching the sunlight. Casey thought back to the endless brides, graduations and children's birthday parties she'd photographed during the past two years. The birthday cake with candles waiting to be blown out, the mother of the bride standing proudly in the receiving line. Treasures to those involved, of course, but to her as a photographer remarkably alike, all of them running together in a blur. Here it seemed a fresh picture was waiting for her at every turn. Even on the way home she'd had to hop off her bike at one point and photograph a field of corn standing in young green rows beside a weathered barn.

"That ought to do it," she said. "See you later, Michael."

She went in through the kitchen door and had just deposited the roses and the bread on the table when the telephone rang. She hurried into the front hall, calling, "I'll get it, Aunt Constance. Don't get up."

"I wasn't going to," Constance replied calmly from the living room. "Nobody I'm interested in talking to at the moment."

Casey grabbed the phone. "Hello?"

"Is that you, Katharine?"

Her father's voice made Casey's spirits plummet unaccountably. "Yes, it's me, Dad."

"Fine. You arrived there all right, then. How do you find everything?"

Casey hesitated. "Aunt Constance is doing quite well. On crutches, of course, but the doctor says—"

"Yes, well, good. Don't forget to send me those X rays. Now, here's the thing. I've been on the phone with the real-estate office up there in—what's the name?"

"Barker Springs."

"That's it. The agent was out of town when I called. Somebody named Nelson. But the office will be getting in touch with you shortly to talk about the property. They're interested, all right."

Dismayed, Casey cried, "But Dad, I was going to do all that myself! And, anyway, I'm not sure yet that Aunt Constance wants to—" She broke off, acutely aware of the woman in the next room.

"Sure, honey, but this will speed things along considerably. Just talk to this Nelson, but don't let Constance sign anything until you've gotten back to me."

"I don't think she's much interested in signing anything, anyway," Casey said, perversely pleased to be telling him so.

"Well, you can help talk her around, can't you? Get that doctor of hers to work on her, too. Laura and Ed are more than willing to have her with them."

Trying to keep the bitterness out of her voice, Casey said, "Will you please just let me handle it, Dad? For once will you let me do something my own way?"

Wright Logan sounded unperturbed. "Sure, sure. It's all yours. Just giving you a little assist, that's all. Call me when there's any news."

"There's one other thing, Dad." Dreading it, Casey knew she had to tell him about her accident. When she'd finished, he sighed deeply.

"Are you sure you're all right?"

"Yes, absolutely. And I've made all the arrangements for the repairs."

"I'll call the insurance company," he said wearily, and hung up.

Casey put the phone down and walked through the living-room archway, trying not to let her frustration show. She was feeling, as she so often did with her father, totally incompetent.

"How's my little brother?" Constance asked airily.

"He's fine." Casey changed the subject. "Pete's Garage will be out here later with a new battery for the truck. You may have to put up with me for a few days, though. Pete said it'll take a while to fix my car."

Constance shrugged.

"I stopped in at Dr. Grant's house, too. I met Mrs. Bates. She sent you some roses and a loaf of bread. Said she'll see you Friday."

"Anna's an old friend."

Casey hesitated, then said slowly, "She mentioned that you'd given Dr. Grant things for his house when he first moved here."

"He gave us a lot too," Constance said, her dark eyes taking on a look of distance and remembering.

"She said something about when he was in California. A wedding that didn't come off. What was that all about?"

"I don't know," Constance said coolly. "I never thought it my business to ask."

I'LL BET SHE DOES KNOW, Casey thought as she strolled across the field behind the house after their early supper. Her aunt, still distant and cool, had made only minimal conversation as they ate, showing no inclination at all to share confidences. Later, when Constance had hitched herself along on her crutches to the front porch and buried herself in a *National Geographic* magazine, Casey had grabbed her camera and set off for a walk. But what difference did the doctor's background make to her? she wondered. Why, after only two days here, was she so interested in him? Was it because he was unlike most of the men she'd known? Certainly her own reactions were new to her. Those other men ran together like the birthday cakes and brides she'd been thinking about earlier. She pictured them at the tennis club, at elegant Washington parties, at fashionable restaurants, exchanging the rumors and stories that always circulated in the city, invariably dressed in the same expensive-casual style. Yet they were faraway and unreal to her now, and all of them seemed to have the same indistinct features. Travis Grant's face, with its strong bones and wide, expressive mouth, kept recurring to her with an almost irritating frequency.

In the meadow, daisies and black-eyed Susans were just coming into flower. She breathed in the heady sweetness of clover as she walked. The sun was still high enough for picture taking, so she headed for a stretch of water she could make out in the distance. She looked back at the weathered barn she'd just passed—it must be the barn Anna Bates had mentioned. Hollyhocks bloomed lavishly at one corner. Casey paused long enough to photograph it, then went on through the tall grass, checking in her bag to make sure she had her zoom lens.

The water, when she reached it, proved to be a good-size pond fed by a small stream and dammed at one end with sticks and mud. The work of beavers, Casey guessed, thinking of Walter. She wondered whether it was an old dam left by some former occupants or whether beavers might be living there now. The pond stood in the midst of a small grove of trees—poplar?— and more of them lined the little stream. She saw sapling stumps and a few dead trees standing in the water.

Using a wide-angle lens, Casey took several shots of the pond as the sun struck it with long golden fingers of light. The dead trees were reflected in the quiet water, and a clump of orange daylilies bent over it. Moving from one point to another, Casey was able to shoot from several different angles and was even able to climb gingerly up on the dam itself. But it seemed solid and well-packed with mud, in no danger of collapsing. Beavers apparently built things to last.

She was sitting down to rest, both arms around her drawn-up knees, when she heard a small rippling of water and saw something swimming toward her. Quickly she reached for her camera; instantly the creature whirled around and swam away. She sat still, and it approached again. A beaver, all right. It stopped a few feet away from her and began slapping the water with its tail so furiously that the first crack made Casey jump. Wa-

ter sprayed in all directions, and the message could not
have been clearer—get out.

"Not until I take your picture, Buster," Casey whispered, digging into the bag for her zoom lens, trying to
make her movements as small and unobtrusive as possible. The beaver fled again, but seemed curious. It circled back, and Casey was able to get several shots before
it took off with another slap of its broad tail. She sat
quietly, waiting to see if the animal would reappear, and
presently it did, with another beaver following. Its mate,
Casey guessed, as she began snapping more pictures.

"Are my friends showing off for you?"

Casey gave a start. Travis Grant had come up behind
her on the dam so silently and she'd been concentrating
so hard on what she was doing that she hadn't heard
him.

"I didn't know they were your friends."

He dropped down beside her. "I come here pretty often—about this time in the evening usually. Used to
come even oftener when I first moved here. Guess I had
more time then. Or maybe I was just lonesome." He
seemed to have lost some of the sharp, critical attitude
he had displayed toward her earlier. Casey thought he
looked more relaxed.

She made a small grimace. "I know what you mean.
I don't feel especially welcome myself."

"Constance giving you the cold shoulder?" he asked,
pulling up his knees as Casey had. "She takes a little
getting used to. I don't think she means to be so stand-
offish, but she's feeling pressured. People manipulating
her life—I suppose that's how it seems to her." Was she
only imagining that some of his earlier remoteness had
faded? Perhaps it had something to do with this place,
where he obviously felt more at ease, more relaxed. Then

he added, "Actually, that's pretty much how it seems to me, too."

So much for mellowing, she thought. She said with deliberate firmness, "No matter what you say, she does need help. If she goes on like this, it's just not going to work. I suspect she's nearly broke already."

"Well, I insist there's got to be another way," he said. "Isn't there always?"

She studied his determined profile, wondering if he was talking about Constance or himself. Then she said hesitantly, "Not to hear my father talk. He called me this afternoon. He thinks there's only one way—his."

"And how do you feel about that?" He wasn't looking at her, but keeping his eyes on the pond. Suddenly, before she could come up with an answer, Casey saw his shoulders tense, his expression sharpen. "Look over there," he whispered. "And don't move."

"What is it?" Casey whispered back. His hand came out to touch her arm as though warning her not to stir. Casey felt a jolting reaction to its firmness and warmth. Then she followed his look and saw a small splashing across the pond where there was a substantial mound of sticks. Both beavers streaked toward it.

"That's their lodge over there," he told her softly. "They're letting the kits out to swim. I think there are two of them. I haven't seen them yet, but I've heard them."

"Heard them?" she kept her own voice as low as his.

"Yes, from inside the lodge."

"Will we really see them?" Casey was tingling with excitement and with the touch of his hand, still lingering on her arm.

"Looks that way."

"Is that another dam?" she asked.

"No, the lodge is where they live and raise their young. Watch."

Two smaller heads appeared as the kits began swimming between their parents. For several minutes Casey and Travis watched in silence as the little family circled and streaked through the water. There was a special intimacy in the moment, and Casey was all the while intensely aware of the man beside her, so close she could feel the warmth of his body. She didn't try to take a picture, fearing she would frighten the animals.

Finally the beavers swam away from them, a hundred yards or so down to the far end of the pond. Casey stood up, stretching her legs, then moving off the dam and onto the bank. Travis followed, and together they stood in the dusky light looking out over the water.

"What happened to those trees?" Casey asked, pointing to the dead trunks.

"They died when the beavers constructed their dam and the water rose."

She frowned. "Are they always so destructive?"

"Yes and no. Actually, certain creatures need rotting trees for their nests—woodpeckers, owls, flying squirrels. So the beavers are helping them. Then later, when the trees weaken and fall, they'll return nitrogen to the soil as they decay. By then the beavers will have moved on to another spot."

She turned to him. "How do you know so much about it?"

His unexpected grin was a sudden warmth between them. "I got elected to the town board of trustees."

She frowned. "And?"

"I found the board pretty heavily weighted in favor of developers, some of whom would love to get their hands on this piece of land, kick the beavers out and build on it. Houses or a shopping mall or whatever."

"And I'm sure you're on the other side." She smiled back at him.

"Well, some of us did begin to feel things were moving too fast. So I began to take time to look around whenever I had a few minutes free."

"And to learn about beavers?"

"Among other things. It was Constance who tipped me off about them. And incidentally, if any of those pictures you took are really appealing, I might ask you for copies to show the town board. I'm not above pulling a few heartstrings in a good cause."

"That's why you don't want Constance to sell," she said.

"You make it sound like an accusation. Yes, that's one reason." A hint of stubbornness crept into his voice. Casey felt herself uncomfortably situated squarely in the middle of the issue.

"Surely you can't put the beavers' welfare ahead of Aunt Constance's," she said in an uncertain voice.

"No, I'm only thinking of what Constance herself wants."

"But you know how impractical she is!" Casey backed away from him, her arms folded across her chest. Then she went on more slowly. "Are we building up to another argument, do you think?"

He moved toward her and said quietly, "I hope not. Because I was just feeling sorry we got off on the wrong foot. And I was also thinking I might want to kiss you."

Before Casey could do more than catch her breath in a gasp, he had covered the short distance between them. His arms were around her, strong yet gentle, pressing her close to him as her face tilted up to his and his lips met hers. Casey, breathless and curiously weak, lifted her arms to encircle his neck and found herself returning the kiss. When they parted, her head dropped to rest in the hollow of his neck. She could smell the fresh outdoor scent of his skin, feel the warm ironed fabric of his denim shirt. She felt safe, protected. If only she could remain there, she thought wearily, forgetting all her problems, renouncing all difficult decisions.

That's the trouble with you, Katharine. She could hear her father's voice, sharp and critical. *You're totally unrealistic. Problems have to be solved, that's all. Now, of course, you have to make your own decisions, but if I were you...*

"I'd better be getting back," she murmured. "Aunt Constance will be wondering where I am."

"Constance isn't much of a worrier." His mouth was touching her hair. She moved then and could just see the pulse beating in his throat. She resisted the impulse to press her lips against it. "Look. They're coming back."

She turned slightly so that she could see across the darkening pond to the four silvery trails made by the beavers as they returned to their lodge. Two furry heads cleaved the water; two smaller ones bobbed between them as the kits swam furiously to keep up. As they approached the lodge they dived and disappeared.

"Underwater entrance," Travis whispered.

Then, so faintly that Casey almost thought she'd imagined it, she heard a tiny whimpering sound. "What's that?"

She heard the amusement in his voice. "I suspect the young ones would like to stay up a little longer. Like kids everywhere. They want the good time to last."

Don't we all, Casey thought wistfully.

CHAPTER FOUR

A SMALL STATION WAGON was just pulling into the lane in front of the house when they returned. In the dusky light they could see an arm waving out of the car's open window.

"Hey, looks like Lee Nelson," Travis said. As they'd walked back across the field hand in hand, Casey had felt a confusion of emotions. A casual kiss wasn't important, she insisted to herself. And it was surely no more than that—a casual kiss. A man as attractive as Travis Grant must have had any number of women interested in him. It would be only natural for him to return that interest now and then. Yet even telling herself this, she couldn't completely calm the excited beating of her heart, the sense that something extraordinary had happened. Now, seeing the strange car in the driveway, she felt a curious letdown. The presence of this other person seemed like an intrusion.

"Lee Nelson? Oh—the real-estate man."

"Real-estate woman," he corrected her. "Didn't you talk with her?"

Casey looked again and saw that the waving arm was slender and pale in the twilight.

"No, I didn't. But I suspect my father must have reached her." Even after she'd begged him not to, she thought crossly. Trying to stop Senator Logan when he had his mind made up was like trying to hold back Niagara Falls.

"Hi, there!" a clear voice called. "Casey Logan?"

Travis and Casey walked over to the car. The woman leaning out the window was dark-haired and smiling, with a smooth oval face and big, almost black eyes. In her late twenties, Casey guessed.

"Casey, this is Lee Nelson," Travis said. "What brings you out this way, Lee?"

"Hello, Casey," the woman said as they shook hands. "Your father called me a little while ago. I've been out of town for a couple of days, and my secretary said he was trying to find me. I was thrilled to hear from him—I've always admired him so much."

Casey, feeling her irritation grow, tried not to let it creep into her voice.

"Yes, I talked with him today, too. I tried to explain that—"

"Oh, I quite understand. He filled me in on the whole picture. Mrs. Pritchard still has to be convinced." Lee Nelson's voice was warm. "I've been waiting a long time to see this property on the market. I know Travis doesn't like the idea at all—" she grinned mischievously at him "—but what I wanted to say to you was, I'm not going to put any pressure on you, or your aunt, either. I really do see the spot you're in. She's holding on because she loves the place, of course."

"Yes, that's exactly it." The sincerity of her tone reassured Casey a little.

"Then we'll have to give her time," Lee said decisively. "And if she does show signs of coming around, I'd like to sit down with her and explain what good use the property would be put to. I mean, I have some really wonderful developers interested. People who'd be sensitive to the environment.''

Casey heard a faint derisive snort from Travis.

"Oh, you're such a cynic, Travis." Lee grinned at him. "But these matters *can* be worked out. Anyway, the important thing is not what I want or even what Senator Logan wants, but what will make Mrs. Pritchard happy."

"I'm really glad to hear you say that," Casey said, feeling easier. "First I have to get to know her better, and then perhaps I'll be able to reason with her."

"Absolutely. And no one should pressure her at all. That's the last thing I want to do." She turned to Travis. "Are you headed home now, Travis? Could I follow you? I'd like to pick up those papers on the rezoning so I can study them before the board meeting, if that's okay with you."

"Sure," he said lightly. "Let's go."

"Casey, you'll forgive me if I run, won't you?" Lee said. "I haven't even unpacked. But I did want to let you know I'll help in any way I can."

Casey nodded and saw them off, watching as Travis slid into the Blazer and waved to her. Then the two cars turned onto the road and drove toward town. Casey stood for a moment before heading back to the house. Lee Nelson and Travis seemed like old friends, comfortable with each other despite their differences. Was Lee interested only in picking up papers for a meeting as she'd said, or was she asserting some prior claim on him? Even if she was, you couldn't really resent someone so frank and likable, Casey thought. Sighing, she made her way over to the disreputable front lawn, past the old truck, now equipped with a new battery, and up the sagging front steps. The air seemed to have turned chilly, and some of the magic had gone out of the evening.

Constance had fallen asleep in her rocking chair on the front porch. Her newspaper had dropped to the floor, and Walter, the tame beaver, was in her lap. Watching her, Casey hesitated for a moment, feeling a sudden rush of compassion. Then she approached her and gently put a hand on her shoulder to wake her.

A SMALL, SLENDER WOMAN carrying a basket of garden vegetables was just entering the kitchen when Casey came down the next morning. Dark hair threaded with gray curled closely against her head. Her bright blue eyes looked lively and intelligent.

"Hi, there," she said warmly. "You must be Constance's niece."

"Casey Logan." Casey held out her hand and the woman shook it, setting her basket on the table first.

"Shirley Townsend. I'm Michael's mother. We live across the road."

"Your son and I have met. He seems like a great kid."

Shirley Townsend looked pleased. "You've hardly left me a thing to do." She made a gesture that encompassed the kitchen.

"It's still pretty jumbled," Casey said. "I don't know where everything goes."

"Oh, Constance likes it like that." Shirley turned to the sink and began running water into a large kettle. "She always says, why put something away in the cupboard when you're just going to take it out again in a few hours? I guess it does make some sense." She picked Bibb and buttercrunch lettuce out of the basket, trimming it and dropping the leaves into the cold water.

Casey switched on the coffeemaker, which she'd prepared the night before. "You work at the hospital, I understand."

"Yes. Housekeeping and maintenance. But when I have spare time I run over here to look in on Constance and do a few things for her."

"She's lucky to have such good neighbors," Casey said.

"We all think a lot of Constance." Shirley sloshed the lettuce leaves vigorously in the water. "Can't imagine her living anyplace but here."

It didn't seem like a pointed remark, yet once again Casey felt uncomfortable, as if she'd inadvertently found herself in the middle of a controversy. She was glad when the phone rang, and hurried into the front hall to answer it.

"Good morning." The sound of Travis's voice made her heart jump into her throat.

"Hi," she said breathlessly.

"I didn't have a chance last night to explain our next move," he said, and she could hear a smile in his voice.

"Our next move?"

"Dinner tonight. I'll pick you up around seven."

"Oh, but... I ought to stay here and help Constance," she said quickly. "I mean, I don't think I should just walk out on her."

"It's Friday night."

"Yes, but—"

"Friday's her social night."

"What does that mean?"

"Means you'd just be in the way there. That bunch of ladies has been meeting on Friday evenings for years. They take turns going to each other's houses, but since

Constance's accident, they meet at her place and bring all the refreshments and such.''

"Anna Bates is one of them?'' Casey asked.

"Sure is. So you and I will clear out before they arrive.''

"Well, if you're sure...''

"I'm sure.'' Casey heard a hesitation at the other end of the line. "You didn't take the X rays with you yesterday.''

Embarrassed, Casey mumbled, "There's no hurry.''

She thought he was about to say something else, but instead he ended the conversation abruptly. "See you at seven.''

Hanging up, Casey felt a tremulous uncertainty, an emotion she couldn't quite define. She needed several minutes to collect herself and adjust her expression before returning to the kitchen.

After Shirley Townsend had put away the freshly washed lettuce and some tiny new carrots, she left for work and Casey took over. Constance hobbled into the kitchen as she was pouring herself a cup of coffee. Casey made them both a breakfast of toast and scrambled eggs, then despite her aunt's protests, she changed the sheets on Constance's bed, collected towels and did two loads of laundry. When the tottering dryer refused to work properly, she hung the wet washing on a clothesline in the backyard, watching the breeze billow it out gracefully.

Later, while Constance settled herself on the front porch, Casey walked through the house, eyeing it critically as she had not had a chance to do before. Notebook in hand, she tried to determine what might need sprucing up if the property was to be sold. Everything, she decided glumly as she forced open a warped door down the hall from the big old-fashioned dining room. This room contained a rolltop desk and some wooden filing cabinets, along with glass-fronted bookcases and an oak swivel chair. Papers were stuffed into every cubbyhole and jammed into drawers.

Casey shook her head helplessly and went back to her aunt, confronting her with this discovery. "It looks as if there might be papers that ought to be gone over, Aunt Constance," she said. "Would you mind if I tackled it?"

Constance was sitting in the fragrant shade of the climbing rose, a basket on her lap, the yellow dog beside her. She was pulling out scraps of material, and the spill of colors was a bright splash against the old gray porch.

"Michael just took Walter to the pond for a swim," she commented, ignoring Casey's question.

"That's nice. What's all that?" Casey nodded toward the scraps.

"Oh, I was just sorting them out. Usually I give them to Anna Bates. She's a wonderful quilter. But I was thinking I might make a quilt myself. I used to do a lot of that kind of thing...."

Casey hesitated, then said, "I met Lee Nelson last night. She drove out here."

"Oh? A smart lady, that Lee. She wants my property, of course."

"She seems pretty low-key. I mean, she wasn't pushing it."

Constance said something that sounded like "Humph."

"She and Travis Grant seem to be old friends," Casey said cautiously.

Constance shrugged.

"Are they more than just old friends?" Casey persisted.

"You'll have to ask them," Constance said with grand offhandedness, and Casey was sorry she'd brought it up. She quickly changed directions. "So is it all right?"

"What?" Constance asked peevishly.

"You know, for me to try to put all those papers in order."

"Oh, who cares? Go ahead. I'm sure you won't rest till you do it."

Casey sighed. She started to turn away, but stopped in midmotion. The colorful odds and ends of cloth lay in a tangle on the older woman's lap, and her strong profile as she bent over them in concentration made a composition of arresting beauty.

"I'd like very much to photograph you, Aunt Constance. Would it bother you?"

Constance didn't look up. "I won't pose, if that's what you mean."

"No, of course not. I wouldn't want you to. Just stay as you are. I'll get my camera."

She returned moments later and began taking pictures, moving around the porch, trying different angles. Constance appeared curiously unselfconscious. She went on calmly sorting the scraps of material in her lap, putting the reds in one pile, blues in another, pausing now and then to reach down and pat the dog beside her. The silence was broken only by the whirring of insects in the grass and the busy humming of bees in the roses. After a time the older woman's hands grew still, and she lifted her head and looked out beyond the house toward a huge old oak tree that shaded the front yard.

"I hated it at first, that was the odd thing about it," she said in a soft voice.

Casey paused, her camera raised, but she said nothing, feeling almost like an eavesdropper. She sensed that the remark had not been directed at her, but was simply a kind of thinking out loud.

"When Frank brought me here, it was his parents' home, that was the thing. I was young, and of course I'd have preferred a place of my own. And I had a mother-in-law to cope with—that bothered me, too. Never occurred to me, of course, that she was having to cope with a daughter-in-law. Young people don't think of things like that."

Casey lowered the camera and held her breath. Constance looked back at the bright scraps in her lap and fingered one that had a pattern of tiny red berries and green leaves.

"We got along, though. That was the way it turned out. One day at a time, you know. It worked out. I had two miscarriages, right here in this house, and she was good to me. Then later, when Frank's father died, she moved to the little cottage. Said it would be easier for her, but I know she wanted us to have the house to ourselves. At the end, though, when we knew she didn't have much longer, I made her come back so I could take care of her."

She placed the scrap of cloth carefully to one side.

"We had a good life here, growing things, fixing the place up. It looked different then, of course. We kept it up better. The seasons came and went and we used to watch them. Frank died here," she finished simply, and then sat still for a moment before returning to the work in her lap.

Casey stood, camera in hand, but Constance didn't speak again, and finally Casey walked quietly into the house and headed toward the little room where she'd seen the piles of papers. She slipped inside and sat down in the old wooden swivel chair at the rolltop desk, leaning forward and resting her head in her hands.

How could she possibly carry out her father's plan when she'd just been given that extraordinary glimpse into Constance's heart? When she knew at last just how much the old house meant to her? Sighing, she lifted her head and pulled the first batch of papers toward her to examine.

Two hours later she sat back, dusty and discouraged. She would've been thrilled to find something—anything—that would help Constance's cause. Casey knew that Uncle Frank had been a tinkerer and a putterer. If this was a made-up story, she told herself, there would have been a patent for an invention amid the clutter. Or a blueprint for some valuable innovation that would have made Constance rich and solved her problems. But to Casey's dismay, all she found were receipts for tax and utility bills, a few modest savings certificates, old bankbooks, an out-of-date driver's license, sales slips from the feed store. And none of them revealed anything except rising expenses year by year.

As she shoved herself away from the desk and got up, Casey grudgingly admitted that her father was right. There was no solution except to sell the place. And at precisely that moment she knew she was going to do everything in her power to prevent it from happening.

AT SIX SHE PREPARED a light supper for Constance.

"No need," Constance fussed. "Anna's sure to bring sandwiches or one of her pies."

"This is just to hold you until they get here," Casey said sternly. "A bowl of soup won't fill you up too much."

"What about you?"

"I'll eat later. I'm going out—with Travis Grant."

Constance's eyebrows rose, and Casey could feel the dark eyes following her as she hurried out of the kitchen. Upstairs, she took a quick bath and washed her hair, then put on a yellow cotton skirt and a yellow-and-white knit top. She dried her hair, brushing it out and letting it hang loose around her shoulders, then slipped her feet into slim sandals. When she came downstairs, she found her aunt and Travis in the living room, talking quietly together. Constance glanced up and gave her an enigmatic look.

Travis's reaction was more forthright. "Well, hi!" His eyes finished the thought for him; Casey's answering smile was half awkward, half pleased. Then there was a momentary flurry as both Casey and Travis saw to it that Constance was comfortable and ready for her guests. Casey had already made an attempt to tidy the cluttered living room and now she herded Walter and the yellow dog, Sarge, onto the back porch.

At last they drove off toward the village in the newly washed Blazer, and Travis, glancing at her, said, "You look wonderful. I hope I've picked the right place for our dinner."

She laughed. "One of Barker Springs's livelier night spots?"

"You might call it that," he said with mock seriousness, and a few minutes later pulled up in front of his own house.

"Do you mind?" he asked, turning to her. "I mean, Anna did most of it—one of her potpie things—and I just thought it would be, you know, a place where we could talk...."

"It's a wonderful idea!" Casey was genuinely delighted. Distance and privacy seemed to have been obsessions with him up to now. Until last night at the beaver pond he'd been almost completely unapproachable. The implication that he wanted them to know each other better caused Casey a shiver of pleasure.

He went ahead of her into the house, leading the way to the kitchen, where a lingering smell of good cooking hung in the air. Everything was spotless; a clean white cloth covered the round table, with a low bowl of pale pink roses in the center.

Travis gestured in a vaguely apologetic manner. "I'm afraid the dining room got turned into my office. We could take our plates into the living room, though, if you'd rather."

"Certainly not," Casey said firmly. "This is absolutely perfect. What can I do to help?"

He gave her a relieved grin. "Let me think now, what did Anna say?" His eyebrows drew together as he concentrated, and Casey looked at them with a small turning-over of her heart. "I remember she mentioned the potpie. And a casserole." He scanned the counter. "There's a note here that says to warm them both briefly. Okay, that's easy. We just have to make a salad."

"Why don't I do that?" Casey suggested. As she assembled salad greens in a bowl she told him about her afternoon in the little office. "I hunted high and low," she said. "Aunt Constance must have saved everything for the last forty years, every scrap of paper, but I couldn't find a thing that would help. I was hoping, I guess, that I'd come across some blue-chip stock certificates she'd forgotten about—anything that would represent some additional capital. But no such luck."

"Hey, wait a minute." He paused in the act of transferring a casserole from counter to oven. "This sounds like a shift in viewpoint. Weren't you the one who was so anxious for her to sell the place?"

"I was," she said, reaching for the celery. "Only I'm beginning to realize now how much it means to her. If there was any way I could help her save it, I would."

"Constance has a way of winning people over," he said.

"My father's not going to like it."

"And you're not used to going up against him." He slid the heavy dishes into the oven and adjusted the temperature.

Casey began slicing a ripe tomato. "Dad likes his own way," she admitted. "It's just that this time I feel I have to— Well, weren't you the one who said sometimes you have to do what's right, not what's easy?"

"I was talking about another situation...."

"Is that why you left California?"

His face flushed slightly. "That has nothing to do with this."

"You said something about going up against power," she persisted.

He shot her a wary glance. "I did what was right for me at the time, that's all." He turned his attention to opening a bottle of white wine and poured them each a glass. Casey finished the salad with a crumble of blue cheese, then wiped her hands and picked up her glass. Over its rim she looked at him. He was standing so close she could feel the warmth of his body, see the broadness of his chest and shoulders, the taper of his long legs. Quickly she took a sip of wine. As she put the glass down, she remarked casually, "Anna Bates said you almost got married. I tried to imagine what she meant."

He frowned and for a moment a muscle in his cheek twitched. Then he shrugged. "Oh, well, this isn't a town that's very big on privacy. Yes, I guess you could say there was almost a wedding. I was engaged, and I came close to having everything I'd always wanted—or so I thought at the time."

"What happened?"

He gave her a long look of gentle irony. "Are you sure you're not an inquiring photographer?"

"All right. So I'm curious."

He sighed and, glass in hand, walked over to the window. "It's a fairly short story. I was on the staff of that big hospital Constance told you about, and I had a difference of opinion with the head of the hospital about who should be treated—or as he thought, who should *not* be treated."

Casey kept her eyes on him.

"One night I was on duty in the emergency room when a father brought in a desperately sick child—only he had no insurance, and I'd been told to send such cases to the county hospital. But I didn't. I treated the child, anyway. Oh, it wasn't the first time I'd had words with the director, but this time it really blew up in my face, and I was let go. Diana, the woman I was engaged to, pleaded with me to let her father intervene. He was on the hospital's board of governors. The only hitch was that I'd have to go along with official policy and be a very good boy in the future." He paused, and she could see the tensing of his shoulders under the white shirt. "So I left."

"I see."

He turned back to her. "It wasn't Diana's fault. It was just that we wanted . . . different things."

"I understand."

He gazed at the floor for a moment, one hand in his pocket. Then he set his glass on the table and raised his eyes to her. "That's the first time I've told anybody about it since I came here. About what really happened, I mean."

And what he'd left out was as clear as what he'd put in, she thought, imagining the unknown Diana's tears and recriminations, the decision that must have been agonizing for him.

"Thanks for listening," he said quietly, walking toward her. She looked up at him, and their eyes held steadily as he bent to kiss her, lightly at first and then with increasing pressure. His arms went around her and his lips sought hers again just as the telephone rang.

"Damn." He smiled wistfully at her, then walked into the hallway to pick it up. She watched him for a moment through the open kitchen door.

"Dr. Grant... Yes, hello, Mrs. Williams ... Why? ... But remember I told you he should take all the medication before ... No, there won't be any problem with side effects ...Call me in two days, why don't you?"

By the time he'd replaced the telephone Casey had already set the casserole on the table and begun slicing through the crisp crust of the potpie.

"Sorry," he apologized. "I get a lot of worry calls."

"Natural enough, if it was a mother, which I'll bet it was."

He nodded, but stopped long enough to switch on the answering machine before returning to her.

"This looks delicious," she said, bustling a little more than necessary as she filled their plates. She was experiencing a sense of confusion about what was happening here. She distrusted her own runaway emotions, but at the same time she felt a pull of attraction between them as strong and fine-spun as a thin wire, which vibrated disturbingly whenever she was near him. "What's in that casserole? Squash, isn't it?"

"I guess so, yes." His eyes followed her.

For several minutes they gave themselves up to the pleasure of Anna Bates's delicious cooking, keeping up a conversation that had to do mostly with the town and its inhabitants. Remembering the attractive real-estate agent and their brief meeting earlier, Casey said, "Lee Nelson seems nice." She hesitated. "I didn't expect her to be so reasonable, somehow."

"Oh, Lee's full of surprises, all right," he said, and Casey couldn't help sending him a quick look, wondering in what ways Lee Nelson might have surprised him. *None of your business, Casey Logan,* she reminded herself.

"What I'd like to do for Aunt Constance," she went on, "is tidy the place up a bit—well, that front yard, for starters. Even if she does eventually come around to putting the property on the market, it wouldn't do any harm."

He shook his head, smiling. "A pretty big job to tackle."

"I know. But it's a great old house. Of course it needs work, but..." She thought about it for a moment. "Well, no matter what, I'm going to make a stab at it. If only to satisfy myself. I want to see what it really looks like."

"There speaks a champion of lost causes," but he smiled as he said it.

"Oh, now, wait a minute! Weren't you the one who wanted her to keep the place?"

"True, and I still do. But my own experiences have made me more of a realist than I once was."

He glanced down at his plate again. Casey studied him for a moment, then she asked quietly, "Who's Dr. Leland Somers?"

His head came up quickly and his forehead showed the lines of a puzzled frown. "What made you ask that?"

"When I was here yesterday Anna Bates said he'd called, and I thought you looked—I don't know—upset."

"Not upset. Leland's a good friend."

"It's none of my business," Casey said. "I shouldn't have asked."

"No, it's all right. Leland's one of the few colleagues who knows what happened in California. There weren't many who thought I was right, but he was one of them. He's recently set up a small hospital in New Hampshire, and he's anxious for me to join him there."

"Are you considering it?"

He didn't answer immediately. At last he said, "I suppose I am. It's tempting. I like Leland—I know we'd work well together. The only thing is, I've had a dream of my own for some time. To establish some sort of health-care facility right here in Barker Springs. Still, his idea is probably a more practical one...." He seemed about to say more, but apparently thought better of it. Casey felt a sudden, surprising pang of disappointment. It really shouldn't matter, she told herself severely. What did his plans have to do with her, anyway? She'd soon be returning to Washington. It was just that Constance would miss him, and so would a good many others in the town. She paused, struggling for honesty.

What she was feeling had nothing to do with Constance, she admitted.

The moment was bridged by the telephone ringing again. This time the answering machine delivered its message and the caller left a name and number.

"Fractured wrist," Travis murmured. "High-school athlete anxious to start physical therapy so he'll be in shape for fall. I'll call him later."

She nodded and they went on eating, sometimes talking, sometimes letting the warm, dusky silence of the kitchen take over. Casey thought of the dozens of dinners she'd had in Washington, sitting across from some man in some smart restaurant. Listening to the hum and buzz of conversation around them as patrons turned and peered at every new arrival, commenting with raised eyebrows and knowing looks. It was a long time, she thought, since she'd felt this relaxed and contented.

"I hope you saved room for dessert," he told her as they both sat back.

"Now he tells me," she said, her eyes rolling upward in mock despair. "I couldn't eat another bite."

"I believe Anna said strawberry-rhubarb pie. She was taking one to Constance and leaving one for us."

"Well, maybe if I work off a few calories washing the dishes."

"Anna won't approve of that at all."

"Never mind what Anna won't approve of. After that heavenly meal she made us, I wouldn't dream of leaving them." She pushed her chair back and began to carry dishes to the sink. He got up to help her, and for several minutes they scraped, stacked, put away leftovers. Then, while she washed, he stood next to her and dried. His nearness made her feel trembly and unsure, and she forced herself to concentrate on the job at hand.

"There. That's the last one," she said finally, drying her hands and starting to turn away. But he was behind her, his arms around her waist, his head bending so that his lips brushed her hair.

"What a lovely woman you are, Casey Logan," he murmured as he turned her around to face him. She looked up at him, her lips slightly parted.

The telephone rang again, and Travis gave a sigh of exasperation. "Having dinner here might not have been one of my better ideas after all," he groaned. They listened as the answering machine dutifully delivered its message but the voice that followed was breathless and panicky.

"Dr. Grant, it's Shirley Townsend. Please call me as soon as you can. It's Michael. He's—I don't know what to do—he's terribly sick—"

Travis was across the room in two steps, scooping up the telephone. "Shirley? This is Travis Grant. What's wrong?"

"Oh, thank goodness you're home. Michael's running a high fever and complaining of a terrible headache. A really awful one. Says he hurts all over."

"I'll be right there." He slammed the phone down and spun around. "Look, Casey, I'm really sorry about this, but it might be serious. I've got to go out there right away."

"I'm coming with you," she said immediately.

CHAPTER FIVE

SHIRLEY TOWNSEND GREETED them at the door, looking pale and shaken. Travis didn't waste words.

"Pains in his abdomen?"

"Yes, and an awful headache." It seemed to Casey that the woman was controlling herself with an effort, anxious to relay all the necessary information to the doctor, determined not to break down.

"Where is he?"

But Shirley was already leading them into a bedroom of the neat little one-story house. There, amid the usual boy's-room clutter of tape player, posters, books, football and a hockey stick propped in one corner, Michael lay sprawled across the bed. Shirley had pulled off his sneakers and placed a blanket over him, but he was still dressed.

"I couldn't even touch him," she said. "Everything hurts. He came in a little while ago, after he'd taken care of feeding the animals for Constance. He looked sick, complained of pains all over."

Travis threw back the cover, carefully examining the boy, touching his arms and legs gently. Then he opened the small bag he'd brought. Over his shoulder he said to Casey, "Call the Addison Mills hospital—Shirley knows the number. Tell them I'm bringing a patient. Intensive care, complete isolation."

"The number's by the phone in the hall," Shirley said in a tight voice.

"I'll take care of it." Casey paused. "Should I say what's wrong?" Her stomach suddenly felt knotted. She tried to draw strength from Travis's own capable manner.

"Meningitis," Travis said tersely, and Casey heard Shirley Townsend's sudden intake of breath. Then Casey fled into the front hall, found the number and made the call. By the time she put the telephone down, Travis was already coming out of the bedroom with the blanket-wrapped Michael in his arms. He went outside and slid the boy, who seemed unconscious, into the roomy back section of the Blazer. Shirley climbed in to sit beside him, tenderly cradling his head in her lap. Travis and Casey got in front.

Trees and houses flew by them in the night as they covered the twenty miles to Addison Mills. No one spoke until they pulled up at the emergency entrance of a trim, modern-looking building where a nurse and two orderlies were waiting with a gurney. Then Travis said softly, "Take care of Shirley, will you, Casey?" and leapt out of the car.

The orderlies took over then, moving Michael out of the car and into the hospital, with Travis giving low-voiced directions to the nurse, and suddenly Casey and Shirley were standing by themselves in the warm June night.

"Well." Casey tried to keep her voice cheerful. "Now that everything's being looked after, why don't we see if we can find a place to have a cup of coffee?"

Shirley, trembling slightly, seemed to rouse herself with difficulty. "Okay." She nodded. "We can go in the same way and... There's a waiting room that..." She seemed to be having trouble finishing sentences, and Casey put an arm around her, feeling Shirley lean on her for support.

Several hours of waiting followed, and innumerable cups of coffee. Shirley, who worked in the hospital's housekeeping department, was obviously well liked; nurses, learning about Michael's illness, stopped to comfort her and offer encouragement. When they were alone Casey did her best to give quiet support without too many words, and now and then Shirley talked.

"After his dad died, Michael was all I had. We didn't have a big family, you see. But it was all right, we managed, and Michael's been so good about helping out. He's been doing yard work and all kinds of things, saving his money for college."

"He's a great kid, Shirley. I know how proud you must be of him."

"Oh, I am. So many young people don't seem to..." Shirley put her coffee cup down and stood up, paced across the room and came back. "I just wonder what's taking so long."

"Well, I suppose there's a lot to be done." Casey had no idea what needed to be done, but still tried to keep her voice light and upbeat.

"Actually I do know something about it," Shirley said. "A case like this, they'll start drips—you know, intravenous—and they might... he might need..." She struggled to steady her voice. "Sometimes they hook a patient up to a heart-lung machine."

"Well then, isn't it lucky you reached the doctor right away and were able to bring him here," Casey said quickly. "This looks like a very well-equipped place."

"Oh, it is. And Dr. Grant's a wonderful doctor. I know he'll do everything he can for Michael. It's just . . . the waiting."

It was after midnight before Travis returned. Casey could almost feel the effort it cost him to put on an encouraging face.

"We've got him all set up, Shirley, full of penicillin and resting like a pasha."

"May I see him now?"

"You bet. Go right in and sit with him if you like. Don't be scared of all the equipment and tubes. You've been around this place long enough to know that's standard. Only before you go in, I have to give you a shot. Already had mine, and Casey, you need one, too."

Casey gave him a questioning look, but submitted meekly, as Shirley did.

"Rifamtin. It's an important precaution," he said, swabbing their arms briskly with alcohol. "Okay now, in you go, Shirley. They'll give you a coat to put on. I'm going to take Casey home and then I'll be back."

Shirley, who'd started down the hall, stopped and turned toward them. "Thanks so much, Casey. For everything."

Casey hurried over to give her a quick hug, then returned to Travis. His expression had sagged into weariness. He rubbed his forehead and then took her arm. "Come on. Let's get you home. This date didn't turn out exactly the way I intended."

"How is he really?" Casey demanded as they left the building.

"About as bad as he could be," he replied grimly. "This disease—the particular bacterial strain he's got— moves fast. I hope we got him here in time, that's all."

"Oh, Travis, if you hadn't picked up the phone ... If you'd been out ..."

"I know. I'm just glad I was there."

"Will you let his mother stay with him tonight?"

"I'm sure I couldn't pry her away." He opened the door of the car for her, then walked around to the driver's side. "Actually, he won't know she's there. He's in a coma."

"Oh, no!"

"Come on. Let's not worry anymore now." He reached for her hand in the darkness. "I haven't had a chance to thank you. Shirley really needed someone tonight. You were great."

"I didn't do anything," Casey protested. "But I'm glad I came along."

"So am I." He held her hand tightly for a moment.

CONSTANCE WAS WAITING UP for them when they arrived. One look at their faces and she said immediately, "Something's wrong. What happened?"

They told her as quickly and gently as possible, and then Travis said he had to return at once to the hospital.

"But he'll get well, won't he?" Constance said worriedly.

"We hope so," was all Travis would say.

"How's Shirley holding up?"

"She'll be all right," Travis said firmly. "Shirley Townsend's tough." Casey wondered if he was trying to convince himself. "It's just that I want to get back there."

"Yes, you must, of course. Let us know something tomorrow," Constance ordered.

"Thanks again, Casey," he said as they waved him off, but at the front door he paused. "You'll be able to manage, the two of you?"

"Certainly," Constance said promptly. "Don't give us a thought."

"I'll take care of the animals in the morning," Casey said. She felt rather than saw the skeptical look her aunt angled her way. No doubt Constance thought she would be worse than useless.

"Can I help you up the stairs, Aunt Constance?" she asked after Travis had left.

"Just carry my crutches," Constance instructed. "I can make it—slowly."

CASEY HAD BEEN DETERMINED to wake up early, so she was dismayed to see full sunlight streaming in the window when she opened her eyes. She seized her watch from the bedside table and looked at it. Already seven-thirty! She jumped out of bed, recklessly pulling on jeans and shirt, dashing to the bathroom and back, quickly brushing her hair. She guessed that Constance, too, was sleeping late; the whole house was quiet as she went hurrying out to the kennel.

The next few minutes were a chaotic mix of barking, meowing and assorted other sounds as impatient animals waited for Casey to measure out dog and cat food from the bins where Michael kept it. She had no idea how much was required, so simply used her own best judgment. Walter tagged after her, almost tripping her up twice, and a little nanny goat pushed in through the door and began nudging her with a determined head.

"Goats!" Casey exclaimed aloud. "What in the world do goats eat?" She gave the animal a gentle shove. "All right. Wait a minute, you. I'll have to look for goat food.''

A shelf on one wall contained bottles and containers of what looked like soaps and medication. One group bore neat labels in Michael's boyish, square handwriting. ''Nick: 1 tsp twice a day.'' And ''Nick: Two tablets with food.'' A large plastic bottle was labeled ''Med. shampoo: Nick.''

With a groan of dismay Casey remembered the little black dog who needed bathing three times a week. She located him in a corner pen, large liquid eyes regarding her trustingly.

''All right, buddy, I'll get to it,'' she promised. ''I guess I can stand it if you can.'' Only first there was the goat to see to and the water dishes to refill. And what about Walter?

Once all the kennel animals were fed, she trudged off toward the barn in back of the house. Goat food, she reasoned, would probably be kept there. Walter lagged behind, attracted by a small birch sapling, which he started to work on. Once she'd fed the goat, Casey told herself, she'd hurry back to start breakfast. Constance should be up by now. She made her way along the narrow path to the barn, feeling suddenly discouraged. All her resolutions of the day before seemed to be crumbling and dissolving like sugar cubes in hot tea. If she weren't here to help out, how could Constance possibly manage in this sort of crisis? Was she really doing her aunt a favor by trying to think of ways to let her keep her house? Wasn't she being, instead, foolishly sentimental? Was her father right, after all? She reached the barn and saw that the door was standing open. A shaft of early sunlight struck the dusty floorboards. Casey stepped inside.

"Oh. There you are. I figured you'd be coming around eventually." The husky voice sounded matter-of-fact.

"Aunt Constance!" Casey stared in consternation at the woman, who sat against one wall of the barn, her crutches scattered in two different directions. The yellow dog, Sarge, stood by worriedly. "What happened?"

"Fell down is all," Constance said. "I was looking for goat pellets, and the damned crutches went out from under me. Couldn't seem to get up again."

"But why didn't you call out?"

"Oh, I was comfortable enough. I figured you'd locate me sooner or later."

"Let me help you up."

"All right, but give Belle her breakfast first. It's in that bucket there. I was just reaching for it when I lost my balance. You can shut her in her pen around the corner of the barn. She always manages to get out."

Casey dumped the pellets into a plastic dishpan and used it to lead the goat into the wire-fenced pen, latching the gate firmly as she left.

"You could have been badly hurt!" she scolded her aunt when she returned.

"Oh, fiddle. Things need doing around here—have to buckle down and do 'em, that's all."

The utter impracticality of it all overwhelmed Casey once again. Her aunt's staying here wouldn't work.

"Hey, where is everybody?"

Casey whirled around as a shadow fell across the barn floor and Travis Grant appeared in the doorway. He was freshly shaven, and his white shirt and jeans looked immaculate, but she could see dark circles under his eyes, and the lines of concern in his face weren't entirely hidden by his determined smile.

"I came through the house. Couldn't find a soul," he said. "What are you doing on the floor, Constance?"

"She fell, that's what she's doing," Casey said severely. "Goodness knows what might have happened if she'd turned that leg under her."

He reached out with both hands, grabbed Constance's and pulled her easily to her feet while Casey retrieved the crutches.

"What about Michael?" Casey asked anxiously as she handed them back to her aunt.

"No change. I just telephoned. Everything's still the same as when I left—that was around four."

"But at least it's not . . . worse."

"No."

"You didn't get much sleep," Constance muttered.

"An hour or so. And a shower helps."

"Tell Shirley we're thinking of her," Constance added quietly.

"Yes, and tell her I'll go to her house and see that things are all right," Casey put in.

"She's worried about her cat."

"I'll feed it. She's not to worry. And why don't I go to the hospital later and sit with Michael for an hour? It would give her a chance to come home and change."

"She might be talked into that. Once people hear about Michael, I'm sure there'll be plenty of help, but for now . . ."

They made their way back to the house and settled Constance safely in the kitchen. At the front door, as Travis left, he pulled her close to him.

"I have to thank you again," he murmured against her hair. "I don't know how I'd have managed all this without you."

"You'd have managed," she whispered back. "And, anyway, thanks isn't what I'm looking for."

"This is sounding better all the time." She lifted her face to his kiss and for a moment he held her tightly. Then he drew away and was gone with a quick wave. Casey stood in the doorway until the Blazer had backed up onto the county road and sped off. Then she returned to the kitchen.

"Well, now," she said briskly, "let's see about some breakfast, shall we?" And after that, she thought with an inward groan, there were vegetables to pick, beds to make and a dog to bathe.

Her aunt was regarding her closely as she measured coffee and poured water into the coffeemaker.

"Anna Bates brought some of her blueberry muffins last night," Constance said. "Why don't we have those...Casey?"

It seemed to Casey that calling her by name had cost her aunt quite an effort, stubborn and proud as she was.

"Good idea," Casey said quietly. "Let's do that, Constance."

The activities following breakfast set the pattern for several days to come, and more than once during the dawn-to-dusk round of work Casey paused to wonder, *what am I doing here? How did all this happen?* She rose early each morning, took care of the animals and cleaned the kennels. She called Shirley twice every day to check on Michael, offering to help whenever she was needed. Several times she drove the old truck into town for groceries, careful not to mention the cost to Constance and paying for most of them herself. She fed the few chickens that Constance still kept, coped with the stubborn goat and took on the special care of nursing the little black dog, Nick, back to health. After the first medicinal bath, which left her drenched and frustrated, she began to manage him better, talking to him and gaining his confidence. Not only did the baths work out better, but she found herself with a new and devoted friend. Now she no longer put him in the kennel with the others, but let him follow her around the house and yard and even sleep on the back porch at night.

"He'll be finding his way to the foot of your bed in no time," Constance observed clearly, not upset at the prospect.

In between her chores, Casey took pictures—of Constance, of the dogs and cats, of Walter and the goat, and of the house. In the back of her mind lurked the idea that if it *did* prove possible to tidy the place up, it would be nice to have a before-and-after record of it.

She seldom saw Travis. She knew he was working around the clock—seeing his regular patients during office hours, then making house calls and stopping daily at the hospital to see Michael. He reported to her often, usually by telephone, only to admit there was no change. Michael was still in a coma.

"Are you getting any sleep?" she would ask.

"Enough. I'll manage."

Casey, who relieved Shirley for an hour or so each day, tried hard to hide her own despair at the sight of the inert boy in the hospital bed. Shirley remained determined, however, and was grateful for Casey's help.

"When he does come to, I want to be sure someone's right there with him. I keep talking to him—Dr. Grant says he may not hear me, but I think perhaps he does."

Often in the evening Casey would walk to the beaver pond and watch the little family out for their daily swim. She'd learned to keep all her movements quiet and steady, even when snapping pictures. She talked to the animals until they seemed to become accustomed to her voice and there was less angry tail slapping. She almost fancied she could see some signs of growth in the two kits.

Then one day after nearly a week had gone by, while Constance was taking her after-lunch rest on the back porch and Casey was in the front yard bathing Nick and had just rinsed him off and wrapped him in a towel, Travis's familiar Blazer came roaring up the drive and stopped with a jerk. Casey's heart pounded uncertainly, but there was something triumphant about the way Travis leapt out and the way he ran over to her, his whole face wreathed in smiles.

"Michael . . ." she said tremulously. "Is it Michael?"

He seized her and spun her around, dog and all, hugging her tight.

"Opened his eyes, recognized his mother and said, 'Hi, Mom.'"

"Oh, Travis!" She put the dog down and hugged him back, then burst into tears.

"Just what Shirley did." He grinned. "Not to mention all the floor nurses. I've been mopping up for the past hour."

"Oh, how wonderful!"

"It's not over yet, of course. If he comes along as I hope, it'll still be the rest of the summer before he even begins to regain any strength. College may have to wait until, well, who knows?"

"And who cares?" Casey added. "As long as he's better."

"We should go out and celebrate," he said, but she shook her head.

"You'd fall asleep over the bread sticks. Come here and eat with us. And be sure to give the hospital our number in case Michael needs you."

"Fine. Okay. I have to get back for office hours now. I'll see you later." He bent and kissed her, held her close for a moment and then was gone. Casey waved until he was out of sight. Then, too excited to go indoors, she began tidying up the yard, a job she'd been meaning to get to all week, picking up loose boards, chains, plastic motor-oil containers and old tires, piling them in a heap, willy-nilly, not working with a plan, but bubbling over with so much sudden energy that she simply had to work it off. From a safe spot on the bottom step of the porch, Nick watched her every move. When she was finished, she loaded everything onto the old truck, whistled for Nick and, with him sitting beside her, drove to the town dump. She was amazed, when she returned, to see how even that small cleanup improved the looks of the place.

"Well!" Constance said, pulling herself out to the front porch on her crutches. "I declare. That *is* better."

Casey, feeling unaccountably pleased and proud, went on working through the afternoon, raking and clearing, yanking at weeds. In the tool shed she located an ancient hand mower, which she cleaned and oiled until it performed surprisingly well. By the time she went inside to bathe and change, the front yard had been cut, somewhat raggedly, but well enough so it looked at last like a real lawn.

Mysterious smells began to drift upstairs as Casey sat soaking in the tub. When she came down moments later, sunburned and full of accomplishment, she found

Constance at the stove, balancing on her crutches but stirring something with determination.

"Beef stew," she announced.

"Oh, Constance, you shouldn't have tried cooking yet! You're not steady enough."

"I didn't try, I did it," Constance declared.

"Well, it smells heavenly. Now you sit down and tell me what to do to finish up. I hope you made plenty—I invited Travis to eat with us."

"I figured you might have. There's enough and then some."

But by six o'clock Travis hadn't appeared. By seven Casey was running to the front windows every few minutes to peer out, watching for him.

"City hours," Constance grumbled. "Nobody eats this late in the country. What's keeping him?"

"You don't think it's Michael, do you?" Casey asked worriedly, returning to the kitchen for the fourth time.

"Well, I suppose it could be, but I don't... Shall we telephone?"

"No," Casey said quickly. "If anything's wrong we don't want to add to it with our questions."

"We could call the hospital switchboard. That wouldn't bother anybody."

"Well, yes, I suppose we could do that."

A pleasant voice at the hospital informed Casey that Michael Townsend was in stable condition.

"I'm hungry," Constance said crossly.

"Let's just wait another few minutes," Casey begged. "Then if he doesn't come, we'll go ahead and save some for him."

But a half hour went by and Travis still hadn't come. In silence Casey filled their plates and sat across the table from Constance. The stew was delicious and she told Constance so, but she found it an effort to eat.

No doubt there was a simple explanation, Casey assured herself in bed that night as she tried to sleep. Doctors had notoriously grueling schedules, were constantly on call, were forever being summoned so that their time was seldom their own. But a quick telephone call would have let her know! She flopped over on her bunched-up pillow. But sometimes it wasn't possible to take even that small extra time, she reminded herself. If someone needed you desperately, then of course you had to... Oh, for heaven's sake, what difference did it make, anyway?

A STOCKY, FRECKLED MAN with strong-looking arms and thinning red hair appeared at the back door the next morning.

"I'm Leo Bates," he announced. "Anna's husband?"

Casey, feeling glum and unsociable after a night of restless sleep, summoned up a smile.

"How do you do, Mr. Bates. I'm Casey Logan, Constance Pritchard's niece."

"I figured. Well, then, I guess you're the one I want to talk to. I work at the milk-processing plant over at Addison Mills, only this is my vacation. And when I drove by here yesterday, I couldn't help noticing the job you were doing, cleaning up the place. So I said to Anna last night, wonder if they'd like me to come with my post-hole digger and make some repairs to that fence of Constance's. I like to keep busy."

Casey pushed open the screen door. "Come in, Mr. Bates."

"Leo," he said amiably. "Be real glad to help out if you think Constance'd be agreeable." Once inside, he seemed to fill up the whole kitchen.

"We certainly could use the help," Casey admitted in a low voice. "Only, the thing is, my aunt's financial situation right now isn't . . . I mean I could pay you something, but . . ." She glanced nervously toward the doorway. Constance hadn't come downstairs yet.

"Oh, shoot, I don't mean for money!" Leo Bates grinned. "It'd just be something to take up my free time."

It was the same kind of answer Shirley Townsend had given her, Casey thought, marveling again at such openhearted generosity.

"I know Constance would be grateful," she said. "What about materials?"

"Might need a few new fence posts is all."

"Well, if you do, I'll pay for them," Casey said quickly. "I can argue it out with my aunt later."

"Good enough. Then I'll go and get started. I brought what I needed in my truck."

"Won't you have some coffee first?" Casey asked.

"Shoot, no, had mine an hour ago." Leo grinned again. "Glad somebody's taking an interest in the place. Hate to see these good old properties go downhill." He banged out the door and strode around to the driveway.

By the time Constance appeared and Casey had explained the project to her, Casey's own mood began to feel a little more cheerful. There had to be, after all, a reason Travis hadn't appeared the night before. He'd been under an extraordinary amount of pressure lately, and the demands of a country practice where there were probably no other doctors to share the caseload must be overwhelming at times. A small voice in her head kept whispering, *But he could have called.* Casey tried not to listen to it.

After breakfast she went outdoors to watch the progress of Leo's work and to continue her own. Weeds had taken over everywhere—along the driveway, next to the house, by the broken fence. Casey began once more to yank and cut, filling her wheelbarrow but leaving anything that looked remotely like flowers. She'd already spotted daisies and black-eyed Susans in what must once have been a border of perennials along the front, and she was leaning down for a closer look at something she thought might be morning glories when she heard a car stop. She straightened and shaded her eyes against the sun. It was Lee Nelson's station wagon, with the real-estate logo on the side, and Lee, slender and stylish in white pants and a loose-fitting navy top, was just getting out.

"Casey! I was driving past yesterday and hardly recognized the place. It looks wonderful!" She pushed sunglasses to the top of her head and looked around her. "Hi, Leo. You're on the project too, I see."

Leo lifted a hand in greeting, then went on methodically thrusting into the earth with his post-hole digger, his pipe in one corner of his mouth.

Casey smiled. "I'm glad you approve," she said, pushing back a wisp of hair. She felt grubby and disheveled beside Lee. "I know you want to put the property on the market, but my aunt still feels reluctant, and I thought in the meantime it would be nice to have it looking a little better."

That wasn't strictly true, Casey admitted to herself. But was there any point in starting a lengthy discussion about her changing attitudes toward the property when she was quite certain Lee Nelson wouldn't understand? And did she entirely understand it herself?

"Of course. Great idea," Lee answered in a friendly voice. "Listen, it can only improve the property, whether she decides to sell or not. I was saying that to Travis just last night."

Something buzzed emptily in Casey's ears and she felt a dryness in her mouth. "Last night?"

"Yes. I know he was supposed to come out here—he mentioned it. That's one reason I stopped this morning, to apologize. But there was this man—Henry Harmon, from downstate. He's thinking of investing in a light-manufacturing plant here, so he came up to talk to the town board. It would do wonders for the town, in terms of taxes and so on. I knew Travis was anxious to discuss the ecological aspects with him. I guess you already realize how obsessed he is on that subject."

Casey nodded wordlessly.

"And since Mr. Harmon was catching a plane late in the evening, it was the only chance we had to see him. So we all had dinner together, and he and Travis talked..." She broke off, studying Casey's face. "Oh, dear. Don't tell me. Didn't he call you?"

Casey shook her head, but flipped her blond braid back quickly in a gesture of dismissal. "Don't worry about it, Lee. It doesn't matter at all. I was only afraid that it might have had something to do with Michael."

"Yes—poor Michael. We've all been worried about him. But, oh, Casey, I feel so guilty!"

"Please don't." Casey managed a smile that she hoped wouldn't look forced. "It's perfectly all right. I'm glad you stopped by, Lee."

"So am I," Lee said warmly. "Well, I have an appointment now—have to dash. Keep up the good work, both of you. The place looks positively spiffy!"

Casey and Leo Bates waved goodbye, and then Leo went on with his methodical digging, shaking his head in amusement as smoke from his pipe curled up around his head.

"That young woman," he said, chuckling. "She's a crackerjack, all right. On the go every minute. I swear, she and Travis between 'em could run this town. Always got their heads together over something or other. Two of a kind, I tell my wife."

"Oh, really?" Casey tried to act unconcerned, but her voice sounded harsh and unnatural in her own ears. *I was saying that to Travis just last night...* She could feel tears prickling her eyes. Turning crossly, she grabbed the wheelbarrow handles and started toward the back of the house with her load of weeds.

A sudden blast of noise split the quiet summer morning as two motorcycles came careering up the road. The men riding them wore T-shirts, blue jeans ripped at the knees, heavy boots, sinister black helmets. They let out wild whoops as they flashed by. Casey dropped the wheelbarrow and shouted for Nick, who was lingering at the side of the road by Leo. The frightened dog came flying to her, and Casey scooped him up anxiously.

"Did you ever— Who *are* those two, Leo?" she demanded.

"Haven't seen 'em before. Must be from over around Addison Mills," Leo said, his placid face darkening with disapproval.

"Well, I wish they'd stay there," Casey grumbled. "A person's not safe crossing the road with people like that on the loose." It was certainly shaping up into a prize-winning morning, she thought glumly. She left the wheelbarrow where it was and went around to the back steps. She put Nick on the porch for safety and was about to leave again when she heard the telephone ringing in the house. Her heart leapt wildly as she hurried inside to answer it.

CHAPTER SIX

"KATHARINE? HOW LONG are you planning on staying there, for heaven's sake?"

At the sound of her father's voice Casey's spirits plummeted again.

"Hello, Dad. Nice to hear your voice, too."

Senator Logan caught the reproach and seemed to make an effort to calm down. "All right, all right. Only we never hear from you. What's going on? I'm up to my ears, and it's going to be very inconvenient for me if I have to come all the way up there myself to get this thing settled."

"You don't have to come here to settle anything," Casey said, speaking with elaborate patience. "Things are going fine. I've been working at getting the place straightened out, looking through Aunt Constance's papers and records..." She kept her statements true but purposely vague. "I've been in touch with the real-estate agent. In fact I was just talking with her a minute ago."

"Well, that's something, anyway," he grumbled. "I know my sister can be difficult."

"She's not difficult at all," Casey insisted. "We're getting along fine. She's just not anxious to sell, and she's not well enough yet to be left alone."

"She doesn't have to be alone, for heaven's sake! She can go to your Aunt Laura's house in Short Hills and get all the care in the world."

"But she isn't convinced yet that's what she wants to do," Casey said cautiously. "I think we should give it a bit more time. And I'm perfectly willing to stay here with her until she's feeling better."

"But not indefinitely," the senator said irritably. "I thought you were going to work on that photography show at the museum this summer."

"Oh. That." The recollection was so far back in memory it no longer held reality for Casey. When she left Washington it had loomed as a major concern—a contest for amateur photographers to be hung in one of the capital's prestigious galleries. She had longed to be a part of it and had even applied for a job to help organize it. "I haven't heard from Mr. Bentley. I sent him a letter with my credentials, but I imagine he's got someone else to run the thing by now. I might as well hang around here for a while."

She could hear the complaint in his voice. "Well, I'd like to see the matter wound up. Constance can't possibly stay there another winter. She hasn't any money and she's getting old." He sighed heavily. "If I have to go there myself to take care of it, I will. I'll just have to rearrange my schedule—"

"No!" Casey shouted into the phone. "Don't come here, Dad, and will you please just leave me alone! I'm handling things fine."

There was a chilly silence at the other end. "I'll overlook that, Katharine," he said at last. "As I said, my sister isn't the easiest person in the world to get along with, I know that."

"Dad, I'm sorry. But you can't manipulate people that way. We have to give Aunt Constance a little more time. Let me stay here and manage things for a while, until she's able to get around better."

He sighed again. "Oh, all right. For a while. But keep me informed, will you, my dear? You could pick up the phone and call once in a while, right?"

"Right, Dad. I will. Love to Mother."

Someone was tapping at the front screen door as she put down the phone in the hall. With a sudden twist of her insides, Casey recognized Travis—saw the broad shoulders, the thumbs tucked into his belt, the long-legged ease of his posture. She went to open the door.

"Hi," she said coolly.

He stepped into the dimness of the hallway. His face was shadowed with concern as he looked down at her, and she was acutely aware of his nearness, his clean outdoor scent, his eyes probing hers. She took a step backward.

"Casey, I'm sorry about last night. I did try to call you, honestly. Several times."

She tried to look unconcerned. "I was outside working all afternoon. And Constance never picks up the phone."

"I was afraid it was something like that. But I just couldn't help what happened. The meeting with Harmon was important—to the whole town. I felt I had to talk to him before it was all wrapped up. Find out what sort of man he is and what his concerns are."

"Oh, I realize you were thinking about the town," Casey said with undisguised irony.

"And by the time we'd finished, it was too late to call you. We had to drive him to the airport at Addison Mills so he could connect with his flight, and then we stopped at the hospital so I could check on Michael."

We. Casey felt anger spilling out like water from an overfull bucket.

"Please don't give it another thought," she said in a stony voice.

"If you could just talk Constance into answering the phone now and then," he said lightly, putting a hand on her arm. But Casey moved away from him. His expression hardened, and after a second's pause he added, "On the other hand, I can't say I blame her entirely. She's probably worried every time it rings that it's another member of your family trying to manage her life."

"Well, at least we're concerned about her!" Casey exploded, but she couldn't help feeling hurt at such an accusation, especially coming on the heels of the altercation with her father.

"Anyway, there's no need to play Florence Nightingale," he said with maddening calm. "The people of Barker Springs would look after Constance."

"Yes, I've noticed what a tight-knit community it is," Casey said in a small, chilly voice. "Outsiders really aren't welcome, are they?"

She could feel his eyes still on her, although she stared at the floor, avoiding his gaze. When she finally did raise her head she could see that he was giving her a long, studying scrutiny. Finally he said, "I didn't know you felt like an outsider, Casey."

Then, before she could answer, he had turned and pushed out through the screen door, taking the steps two at a time and striding across the lawn toward the Blazer parked in the driveway.

Casey hurried blindly back through the house and out to the back porch. She could hear Constance humming softly in the vegetable garden as she leaned forward on her crutches to examine the progress of the tomato plants. Casey sank to her knees and put her arms around

This lovely Victorian pewter-finish miniature is perfect for displaying a treasured photograph. And it's yours FREE as added thanks for giving our Reader Service a try!

Harlequin Reader Service® Sweepstakes Entry Form

This is your **unique** Sweepstakes Entry Number: 5U 378084

This could be your lucky day! If you have the winning number, you could be the Grand Prize Winner. To be eligible, *affix Sweepstakes Entry Sticker here!* (SEE OFFICIAL SWEEPSTAKES RULES IN BACK OF BOOK FOR DETAILS.)

If you would like a chance to win the $35,000.00 prize, the $10,000.00 prize or one of the many $5,000.00, $1,000.00, $250.00 or $100.00 prizes . . . plus the fabulous Bonus Prize—two new Cadillacs and the Deluxe Hawaiian Vacation . . . *affix Prize Sticker here!*

To receive free books and gifts with no obligation to buy, as explained on the opposite page, *affix the Free Books and Gifts Sticker here!*

Please enter me in the Sweepstakes and, when the winner is drawn, tell me if I've won the $1,000,000.00 Grand Prize! Also tell me if I've won any other prize, including the cars and the vacation prize. Please ship me the free books and gifts I've requested with sticker above. Entering the Sweepstakes costs me nothing and places me under no obligation to buy! (If you do not wish to receive free books and gifts, do not affix the FREE BOOKS and GIFTS sticker.)

116 CIH AGMF
(U-H-R-09/92)

YOUR NAME   PLEASE PRINT

ADDRESS   APT #

CITY   STATE   ZIP

Offer limited to one per household and not valid for current Harlequin Romance® subscribers.   © 1991 HARLEQUIN ENTERPRISES LIMITED

HARLEQUIN'S "NO RISK" GUARANTEE

- You're not required to buy a single book—ever!
- As a subscriber, you must be completely satisfied or you may cancel at any time by marking "cancel" on your statement or by returning a shipment of books at our cost.
- The free books and gifts you receive are yours to keep.

ALTERNATE MEANS OF ENTRY: Print your name and address on a 3″ × 5″ piece of plain paper and send to: Harlequin's Wishbook Sweepstakes, 3010 Walden Ave., P.O. Box 1867, Buffalo, NY 14269-1867

Nick, who'd immediately trotted up to her with his wet nose and inquiring eyes.

What had made her lash out in such a petty way? Of all the silly emotional outbursts! And over something completely unimportant. Hot tears spilled down her cheeks and she brushed them away angrily. Why were things turning out like this? Why was she suddenly losing control? Most of all, why had she let Travis Grant become that important to her?

Half an hour later, her face washed and her feelings under better control, she walked out to admire the work Leo Bates had done on the front fence. She picked up two crumpled beer cans that had been tossed at the side of the road and thought again of the bikers who had gone roaring by earlier.

"A fairly busy morning around here," Constance commented at lunchtime. "Anything important?"

Casey busied herself with the whisk, beating eggs for an omelet. "No, nothing important."

THAT EVENING after she'd helped Constance get comfortably settled with the newspaper in her usual spot on the front porch, Casey slipped out the back. All through dinner she'd been half listening for the telephone, and the meal itself—leftovers from the night before—had been an abrasive reminder.

"I always think stew tastes better the second day," Constance murmured, but Casey only nodded indifferently.

Now, walking out into the long rays of the late sun, Casey started from habit toward the beaver pond. She had left Nick enclosed, unhappily, on the back porch, fearing he might offend the beavers. But after a moment's thought, she changed course and went in the opposite direction, toward a small cluster of trees on the other side of the property where she hadn't explored yet. Constance had mentioned a cottage, and Casey knew it lay there among the trees, for she'd caught a distant glimpse of it. A narrow, overgrown path led to it. In the little grove were long fingers of dappled sunlight, and among the weedy undergrowth some signs that there had once been a garden.

The cottage, when she came upon it, had a snug, close-to-the-earth look, with a long low roofline and mullioned windows. It needed paint, as did the main house, and Virginia creeper had twined itself around the chimney and insinuated itself into the gutters. Casey tried the front door—locked, of course. Feeling around the frame with her fingertips, she found a key hanging on a rusty nail. She turned it in the keyhole and pushed the door open cautiously, then tiptoed inside. Furniture was covered with sheets, and there was evidence of mice and busy spiders, but it was less rundown than she'd anticipated. She walked around slowly, exploring. The place seemed to have two rooms. The one she'd entered was part living-room, part kitchen. A small sink and gas stove were at the far end, along with cupboards. A fireplace was built into the opposite wall. A door led to a tiny bedroom with a four-poster bed, a small chest of drawers and a washstand.

Casey returned to the main room, brushing down cobwebs and pausing here and there to pull back a dust cover and look at what lay underneath. All the furniture seemed surprisingly sound except for one small chair cushion chewed open to make what appeared to be a mouse home. For a moment she stood in the middle of the floor, thinking. Then she went out, locked the door and replaced the key, and hurried back to the house.

The light had dropped lower, but Constance was still sitting on the front porch in the dusk when Casey came up the steps.

"Constance, I was just exploring, and I found the cottage back in the woods."

"It wasn't really lost, you know," Constance said dryly.

"Well, I'd never happened to walk that way before. It's a beautiful little place!"

"Used to be a hired-man's house. Back when the farm was bigger. Later, when we didn't need a hired man anymore, we fixed it up better for Frank's mother, put in a bathroom—I told you that, didn't I? That was the last time anybody used it."

"Is anything wrong with it?"

Constance shrugged. "Might be a little leak at the kitchen end. I seem to remember that. Roof probably needs patching."

"But nothing else?"

"Nothing I know of. Chimney might want repairing, although maybe not—that fireplace was added later, when we put in the bathroom."

Casey took a deep breath and pulled a chair over beside her aunt. Sinking into it, she asked, "Could we fix it up? Paint it and ask Mr. Bates to help patch the roof?"

"What for?"

Casey let her breath out softly. "We could rent it."

Constance gave her an unbelieving look. "Who'd rent an old rundown place like that? And how would we ever pay Leo?"

"You haven't been keeping up, Constance. Old rundown places like that are a very big item these days. Back to basics, the country look—there's a demand for it. It would be perfect for a young couple. And income for you. Also, if you had someone living right here on the property, you wouldn't be alone anymore, would you?" Casey's mind was racing through the possibilities. "As far as Leo's concerned, I'm sure he'd be willing to let us pay him a little at a time." Privately, Casey doubted that Leo would accept anything at all.

"You mean . . ." Constance was thinking about it, turning the notion over in her head. "Maybe renting the cottage might be a way to . . ."

"Maybe," Casey said. "It just might be."

A slow smile formed on the older woman's face. "My brother," she said thoughtfully, "would blow his stack."

"Oh, come on now," Casey said, trying to summon up family loyalty. "Dad would be pleased if you found a good solution."

"Not if it wasn't his solution," Constance said, but her voice was beginning to sound hopeful. "Is it worth a try? Do you really think so?"

"I'll take Mr. Bates over there in the morning and ask his advice on what needs to be done."

Too excited to settle down, Casey wandered around the house and the yard for several minutes, then brushed Nick vigorously, noting how his mangy coat was already turning glossy, the bare spots filling in. She hugged him and left him on the porch for the night before returning to Constance and helping her up the steps to bed. Only when she'd crawled into her own bed did some of that morning's pain return. Travis's hurt look as he left her, the apologetic sound in his voice, her own curt refusal to bend. Why had she been so stiff and unforgiving? But on the other hand, wasn't she at least partly right? She thought again about the cottage and what it might mean to Constance. What it might mean to Casey

Logan was another matter entirely. She could leave, all problems solved, and Travis and Lee, with a world of common interests between them, could pick up where they'd left off.

Unhappily Casey turned her head into the pillow and tried to sleep. It was some time before she dropped off, however, and the last thing she heard before she slept was the roar of two motorcycles tearing past on the road. She slept fitfully, and once during the night she heard barking from the kennels.

She woke up feeling dull and lethargic, cross because these restless nights seemed to be developing into a habit. She dragged herself out of bed, dressed and went downstairs, pausing in the kitchen long enough to start the coffee. Then she went to the back porch with Nick's breakfast before heading for the kennel and the other animals. The porch was empty, the gate she used to enclose it wrenched open crookedly.

"Nick?" Casey felt a shock of panic as she dashed down the steps. "Nick!" There was no sign of the little black dog, but several other dogs were waiting for her, all with eagerly wagging tails, and in the vegetable garden Belle, the goat, was tramping on young runner beans and munching on Constance's tomato plants. The wire fence around the garden had been ripped away. Furious, Casey ran toward the goat with arms swinging, shouting at her and finally steering her out of the garden and back toward her own penned-in area by the barn, where the fence had also been torn down. Casey fastened her temporarily with a length of rope and dashed toward the kennel, with several dogs trailing after her. There she saw that the door to the kennel house had been yanked off one of its hinges. Inside, the wire barriers that separated the kennels had been torn down.

She came back outside, anger bubbling rapidly to the surface. She counted the dogs. Some of them were already trying to push past her to get inside again, recalling where the food was. Seven, eight, nine—all accounted for, except Nick. Walter was happily working away at his pile of brush, gnawing on a good-sized branch. Three cats missing, but those would turn up, she felt sure.

She gave the dogs their food, wedged the door shut behind her and went to see if the fence enclosing the outdoor runs was intact. It, too, had been pulled down, but less viciously. She was able to prop it up and pound the supporting stakes back in with a hammer; they'd hold temporarily, she figured.

Leo Bates had arrived by the time she was finished. He stood with hands on hips, scowling angrily at the new fence posts he'd installed the day before. They had been too solidly planted to be budged, but several of the cross rails had been broken.

"It gets worse," Casey said grimly, describing the rest of the damage. As she talked she kept looking around, hoping to see a glimpse of Nick.

Leo Bates shook his head. "Never saw the like," he muttered. "Got to be those two hoodlums."

"The motorcyclists?"

"Who else?"

"But why would anybody do such a thing?" Casey wailed.

"Looks like just pure cussedness to me." Leo, still shaking his head, was taking his toolbox out of his truck. "Better start with the kennel, I reckon. You call the sheriff?"

"No—I've been busy rounding up the animals. I will, though. You didn't see any sign of a little black dog, did you? He's the only one still missing."

"Didn't see him. He'll probably show up." Leo was already on his way to the kennel.

For a moment Casey stood there, disconsolate and alone. She took one last look around, whistling and clapping her hands. Then she returned to the house to telephone the sheriff.

"What is it, Casey?" Constance had stepped out onto the front porch wearing a voluminous blue housecoat and one fuzzy pink slipper. Her long hair streamed down her back and her face was pale and anxious as she balanced on her crutches. "I heard a lot of commotion. Did the dogs get out?"

As gently as she could, Casey explained what had happened. Constance's face grew even paler, then flushed with anger.

"I was just coming in to call the sheriff," Casey finished.

Constance took a deep breath and whispered, "Damn. If I just didn't have to depend on these things..." She jiggled the crutches impatiently. "All right, you come into the kitchen and have some breakfast. That's the first thing, and no back talk. I'll get hold of the sheriff. Then I'll make some calls to neighbors along the road, see if anyone's seen Nick."

Casey started to protest, but Constance was adamant, and Casey felt her aunt's decisiveness, her determination. She'd been thinking of her only as someone hurt and in need of help, but obviously Constance possessed reserves of strength Casey hadn't seen yet.

"Leo thinks it might have been those two guys on bikes. Did you hear them tearing past yesterday?"

"Yes." Constance seemed to be considering it. "Possibly. We'll get to the bottom of it," she added briskly, and with far more spirit than Casey was feeling at the moment. "You're sure everybody's accounted for? All the dogs? What about Walter?"

"All there except for Nick. Three cats missing, but they'll probably show up."

"I'm sure they will. Cats are smart enough to stay out of the way till things calm down."

As if to prove her prediction, there was a mournful meowing from the back porch, where a large tiger cat was hanging onto the screen door, spread-eagled and complaining. Two others, one orange and one black-and-white, sat on the steps voicing their own complaints.

Casey's eyes darted past them, but no sign of Nick.

"All right," Constance said, still sounding decisive. "Breakfast first. We'll feed the cats right here."

Casey left her, a half hour later, sitting by the telephone with a list of numbers in her hand. Her strong voice followed Casey out. "Constance Pritchard, Sheriff. We've had some trouble out here at my place...."

Leo had already rehung the door of the kennel when she returned. Several dogs, delighted with the unaccustomed confusion, were capering around his legs, and Casey eventually managed to shoo them inside and to help Leo put the fence back securely around the outdoor runs. They were just heading toward the goat pen when Travis Grant's Blazer nosed into the driveway. Casey, her heart leaping, stood still, watching, while Leo plodded ahead, toolbox swinging from one hand.

It took Travis a moment to get out of the car, and when he did he backed out, shutting the door with one foot as he balanced an awkward bundle.

"Are you missing someone?" he called out, walking toward her with Nick in his arms.

Casey gave a small cry and ran to him, taking the dog from him, hugging Nick close and feeling a warm tongue licking her face furiously.

"Where did you find him?" she asked through joyful tears.

"Slogging along the road a mile or so back, completely lost and tired out. What's been going on here?"

Briefly she filled him in, pointing out the vandalism. "Leo thinks it must have been bikers from Addison Mills. Constance called the sheriff."

He was frowning, looking around with a clenched, angry expression. "The other dogs didn't run off?"

"No, they stayed close to the food, I guess."

He glanced at Nick. "I don't think he ran off, either. I think he was taken somewhere and dumped."

"Oh, no." She hugged the little dog tighter. "Who would do such a heartless thing?"

"None of this showed much heart," he commented, and the two of them were silent for a moment. Then he said, "Look, Casey, is there anything at all I can do to help?"

Feeling suddenly embarrassed at the emotion she'd shown, Casey shook her head silently. She had no wish to depend on him again for emotional support, to let him become important to her. She'd allowed that to happen before, and it had been a mistake.

"We're fine," she said, keeping her voice steady. "Constance is running things from the telephone, and Leo and I will have the place back in shape in no time. I know how busy you are. What about Michael? How's he doing?"

"Stronger all the time, although as I told you, it's going to be a long business."

"Tell Shirley I'll stop by as soon as I can."

"I'll explain that you're pretty busy." They talked together politely, but as casual acquaintances now, all their former intimacy gone.

"Thank you for rescuing Nick," she said as he got back into the car. He lifted his hand in reply, and Casey, turning away, could feel his eyes on her for several seconds before she heard the Blazer drive away.

Well, she thought, trying to be sensible, *things worked out for the best, didn't they?* Better to get it straight between them now. Later, when she went back to Washington, it would be easier all around, wouldn't it? But the ache that had settled around her heart refused to budge.

Working alongside Leo Bates all morning was a welcome activity. Between them, they straightened fences, pounded stakes, replaced splintered rails. Leo also repaired the gate so Nick could once again be enclosed on the back porch. But even though it looked sound, Casey decided privately to take Nick upstairs with her at night.

Around midday, just before Leo packed up his tools to leave, Casey led him back to the little cottage and asked his advice on repairing it. Leo relighted his pipe and strolled around, tapping and poking, looking at pipes, turning on faucets and examining a small brown spot on the ceiling of the kitchen area.

"Bit of a leak there," he remarked. "Nothing much. I'll bring some new shingles tomorrow and patch it."

"Oh, would you, Leo? And can I go ahead and buy paint? Start cleaning the place up?"

He grinned and puffed. "Can if you don't mind a messy job of work."

"I don't mind."

CHAPTER SEVEN

THE HARDWARE STORE was her first stop when she drove into the village that afternoon. She spent some time looking at color charts before deciding on a soft gray-green for the interior of the cottage, then outfitted herself with brushes, rollers, paint trays and buckets and lugged everything out to the truck. Next she went to the drugstore where two days before she'd left pictures to be developed. She took them out of the envelope and smiled as she looked at them, then walked up the street to a building with a grubby-looking front window and the words *Barker Springs News Leader: Since 1923*.

She had approached Constance over breakfast with an idea that had been brewing in her head along with the plans for renovating the cottage, and was both pleased and surprised that Constance agreed to it almost at once. It was as if, having opened the door to one innovative idea, Constance was willing to let others in.

As she entered the newspaper office, Casey saw a woman on the telephone at a counter facing the front door. Behind her stood four desks with word processors and farther back a large drafting table. All the desks were occupied, and at the drafting table a man was bent forward, laying out a page. The whole place had an air of cheerful confusion.

"Yes, may I help you?" The woman at the counter put down the telephone.

"I'd like to see the editor," Casey said.

Another woman got up from one of the desks. Her sandy hair stuck up as if she'd just run her fingers through it. She looked at Casey over glasses that had slid partway down her nose.

"I'm Joan Singleton," she said. "I'm the editor."

Casey introduced herself and brought out the handful of pictures. "I was wondering whether I could interest you in a weekly feature. Pet-of-the-Week or Adopt-a-Pet or something like that. My aunt and I think it's an idea that might catch on."

The woman adjusted her glasses and gazed at each picture in turn, letting out small exclamations, and now and then laughing. "Sandy, look at these." She showed them to the woman at the counter. "Eddie! Come here a minute," she called over her shoulder, and the man in back got off his stool at the drafting board and ambled over. He was long and lanky, and his glasses were sliding down his nose just like hers. "This is my husband, Ed Singleton," she explained. "He handles our advertising. And a little bit of everything else. Look there, Eddie."

"That's got to be out at Constance Pritchard's place," the man said with a grin.

"It is," Casey said. "I'm Casey Logan, by the way. Constance's niece."

"These sure look professional. Are you?"

"Professional? Well, yes. And if I'd been able to do the developing myself, I'd have cropped them differently, but you get the idea."

They spread the pictures out on the counter and bent over them, talking for several minutes. Then Casey shook hands with both of them and left, climbing back into the truck and this time heading for Elias Kelsey's feed store on the edge of town.

The usual group of regulars was on hand, and all of them greeted Casey warmly. She waited for Elias to finish with a customer before engaging him in conversation and presenting him with her proposal. Would he be willing to give a discount on dog food to anyone adopting one of Constance's strays? The Singletons would mention his store in the new weekly pet column, she told him. Elias agreed readily. On her way back to the truck, she couldn't resist stopping at a bright display of plants just outside the door, and when she came back in with a flat of pink impatiens, she was followed by Pete, the garage owner, who had just arrived.

"Woulda had that car of yours fixed this week, ma'am, only I had to replace the gas tank—remember I told you that?—and they sent me the wrong one. I got the right one now—oughta be done pretty quick," he promised.

Casey assured him she was in no hurry.

"Well, good thing," he said, "because the wife's got me running around like crazy helping her with all the arrangements. Daughter's getting married soon, and you never seen such a to-do. Plan is to have a party in the backyard after the church, but what if it rains? my wife says. So I had to paint the dining room just in case." He laughed and shook his head.

"Is someone taking pictures of the wedding?" Casey asked.

"Oh, shoot, that's another thing," Pete said, slapping a greasy palm against his forehead. "Got to pick up film for the camera."

Casey hesitated. "Would you like me to take some pictures for you?" she asked. "That's what I do—I've photographed a lot of weddings. No charge," she added hurriedly. "Your wife and daughter might like it."

"Say, would you do that?" Pete beamed happily. "Take a load off my mind. But not for free, now. I'd be glad to pay."

Casey set her plants on the counter and dismissed the offer with a wave of her hand. "I'd enjoy doing it," she said, and realized she really meant it. Odd that she was planning ahead this way when she'd originally intended to spend only a few days here. And somehow the prospect of this small-town wedding was more attractive to her than the many lavish affairs she'd photographed in Washington lately.

Pete produced a greasy scrap of paper and a stubby pencil and jotted down the name of the church and the address of the house, along with the date and time. Casey took it and had just turned to pay for her plants when she was stopped by the sound of voices coming from somewhere in the back of the store, behind one of the many piles of feed and seed.

"No, I think you should all come to the next meeting. There are things you should know about," an unmistakable voice was saying. Casey, holding the flat of impatiens, was torn between the impulse to edge out quietly before she encountered Travis and a certain fascination with what he was saying.

"We need the industry, Doc," another voice put in.

"Sure, I know it. And I think this fellow's okay. I got a good impression of him. But there are questions to be asked. And once he's established here it'll be a lot harder to get answers."

"Bring a lot of jobs in," someone else said. "We all want that."

"But not if you find it's ruined your favorite trout-fishing spot."

"Why should it do that?"

"Shouldn't, if we make sure the necessary precautions are taken. Anyway, you'd better all come and meet him next time he's in town."

Casey moved toward the door, backing up to it with both her hands occupied. But it was latched, and she was obliged to balance the flat on one hip while she fumbled at the doorknob with her free hand.

"Let me do that."

She looked up into blue eyes and the smile that always seemed to make her heart flip wildly.

"Oh...thanks. I was just...I seem to have been doing some impulse buying," she murmured.

He held the door open for her, then took the flat and walked with her toward the truck. Casey kept her eyes averted.

"Casey," he said softly. "We're not enemies, are we?"

She felt a blush rise to her cheeks and forced herself to look at him.

"Of course not." She felt suddenly foolish for avoiding him and said lightly, "Well, this place certainly is the nerve center of Barker Springs. I just made an appointment to photograph a wedding."

"Oh? Pete Ridley's daughter, I'll bet. Great. I was doing some campaigning myself. Trying to whip up a little more involvement on the part of the citizens." He slid the flat into the truck's passenger seat and whistled as he saw the paint supplies. "Good Lord, what's all this?"

"Well, I—I'm planning on doing a little redecorating."

"Constance's house?"

"Not exactly. The cottage back in the woods." Briefly she outlined what she had in mind.

His eyebrows went up and he grinned admiringly. "For somebody who was awfully anxious to sell that property, you're going to a lot of trouble to try and save it."

She felt suddenly shy and glanced away from him. "I only want what's best for Constance."

"And your ideas on that score have changed?"

She looked back at him and their eyes locked.

"Let's just say I'm exploring options." She opened the door and climbed into the truck, then smiled back at Travis. "And thank you again for returning Nick. I've gotten awfully attached to him."

He folded his arms in front of his chest. "How do you think he's going to like Washington?"

She hesitated. "I haven't really thought that far ahead."

"Best thing," he said gravely, but with a twinkle in his eyes. "One day at a time."

"I'm UP HERE," Constance called from overhead when Casey came in. Ordinarily Constance never went upstairs during the day, declaring that once at bedtime was enough to cope with the steps. Now, however, Casey found her in her bedroom, hobbling from closet to bed and looking mildly distraught. A pile of clothes was spread out on the bed, and Constance was holding some sort of blue garment in one hand.

"What is all this?" Casey demanded.

"That Anna Bates," Constance fussed. "Won't take no for an answer. Here it is Friday again, and she insists I'm well enough now to go out. So the girls aren't coming here—nothing will do but Anna's to pick me up and take me to her house. I haven't been anywhere in weeks—what should I wear? Last time I went out it wasn't even spring yet.''

Casey maintained a serious face even though she was tempted to smile at Constance's mention of "the girls" and her concern over her wardrobe. She approached the bed, glancing at the helter-skelter pile.

''What would you wear if they were coming here?''

''Oh, any old thing.'' Constance made a sweeping motion with the hand holding the blue dress. ''It's different when I'm here. This is my house.'' The argument seemed to hold some logic for her, so Casey refrained from arguing. Instead, she gently removed the dress from Constance's grasp.

''How about this one? It's a pretty shade of blue.''

Constance studied it doubtfully. ''Needs pressing,'' she said. ''And look, there's a tear in that seam at the side.''

''I'll fix it,'' Casey said firmly. ''Just relax, Constance.''

By the time Anna Bates arrived to pick her up at seven o'clock, Constance was wearing the pressed and mended blue dress, her hair neatly brushed. The shoe on her good foot, in place of the fuzzy slipper, seemed oddly unfamiliar. Her eyes were bright with excitement as Casey and Anna helped her into the car.

''Don't wait up for me,'' Constance tossed over her shoulder as Casey waved her off.

Alone in the house, Casey wasted no time, but made herself a sandwich, then hurried to assemble her painting materials, eager to get the cottage project under way. She had just changed into jeans and an oversize shirt when the telephone rang. She dashed to the front hall to answer it.

"Katharine? Now don't get huffy about my calling again." Her father's voice held a mock-defensive tone. "I have some news this time."

Casey had to smile in spite of herself. "All right, Dad, what is it? I'm on my way to paint a house."

There was a moment of silence, but the senator apparently decided to let the remark pass. "I had a call this afternoon from Harrison Bentley's office. He wants you to direct that museum show. Wants to mount it this fall and says the sooner you get at it the better."

Casey swallowed, feeling stunned. "He wants me? To direct it?"

"Well, manage it, whatever you call it. Wants you to run the thing, help judge the entries and so on."

Casey's head swam. A month ago she would have been euphoric about the prospect of directing such a prestigious show. Even now she was thrilled, yet she felt herself pulled in two opposing directions. Her aunt's situation had involved her in a way she wouldn't have thought possible when she'd first arrived here. And Travis Grant... She took a deep breath and steered deliberately around *that* issue.

"But I wrote him ages ago," she protested. "I can't imagine why he waited so long to decide he needed me."

Senator Logan cleared his throat. "Well, as it happens, by the purest coincidence I was having lunch with him today and the matter came up, just by chance of course—"

A familiar anger flared up in Casey. "Dad! Did you do some arm twisting over this?"

"Absolutely not. I merely asked him how the plans were shaping up and he mentioned your application. It seems to have impressed him."

"No pressure applied?" Casey asked severely.

"Absolutely none, I swear. Make no mistake, my dear—Harrison Bentley doesn't react kindly to pressure, political or otherwise. He wants you."

Wavering, wondering, longing to believe him, Casey said uncertainly, "I couldn't come for a couple of weeks. It'll take me that long to wind things up here."

"He'll be getting in touch with you. You can discuss it with him then."

Excited yet bewildered, Casey turned back to the job at hand, glad to have an outlet for the sudden burst of adrenaline surging through her. Had her father put pressure on the museum director at that luncheon meeting? Much as he denied it, Casey harbored an uneasy suspicion. But she did know Harrison Bentley, knew him to be a strong, opinionated man, not the type to knuckle under to politicians. So if he really *had* picked her—if he really wanted her... She dashed back to the kitchen where paint and rollers awaited her in a pile by the door.

It took three trips to the cottage, lugging buckets, brooms, and finally a stepladder. By then the light was fading. Casey had already tried the switch and found that the overhead light in the living room worked, so she was able to start sandpapering the walls wherever she found rough spots, preparing the surface for paint. Nick, who had made every trip with her, explored with wild curiosity for a few minutes before settling down in a sheet-covered chair.

As the shadows drew in, Casey made a deliberate effort to keep recollections of her father's phone call from intruding. Excited as she was over the idea of the show, she felt reluctant to make a decision about it. Barker Springs and her aunt's problems had become such an important part of her life these days. And then there was the matter of... She pursed her lips hard and tried to hold at bay thoughts of Travis Grant and what he had come to mean to her lately. But no, that was over. There was no involvement there, she reminded herself. It was all working out for the best. Yet in spite of her efforts, reminders of him kept coming, and his quick smile, the laughter in his blue eyes as he'd looked at her today, imprinted themselves on her mind so that she saw them in front of her while she worked. She busied herself opening the first bucket of paint, stirring, testing, trying it out on a small spot; then she began applying it with a roller to the wall opposite the fireplace.

None of that mattered, anyhow, she told herself sternly. What mattered was what she could do to help her aunt—never mind whether or not her father approved. And the intelligent thing would be to conclude the business here as soon as possible, get back to Washington and take up her life where she'd left off. Now that she had this offer from the museum it was all much clearer. Casey squared her shoulders, took a deep breath and had just dipped into her paint tray again when she heard a knock on the door. Nick let out a short yip and sat up, and Casey felt a sudden tremor of anxiety as she thought of vandals, strangers and the lonely woodland setting. She put down her roller and approached the door cautiously, Nick crowding her heels.

Inching it open, she saw Travis Grant standing there in worn jeans and an old plaid work shirt.

"Thought this was where I'd find you." He smiled. "I came to help." Nick slid out the door and jumped around him happily. "Unless," Travis added with a nod toward the little dog, "you have all the help you need."

Casey's breath caught in her throat. For a moment she was speechless, trying to grab hold of her list of reasons for not getting involved, trying to remember what it was that she had just decided was the sensible thing to do. Slowly she opened the door the rest of the way. His eyes were on her, as blue and direct as she remembered, and his mouth was quirked in a tentative smile.

"Well, I guess . . . I mean, we can always use another hand, can't we, Nick?" Nick gave a final excited leap, and then, deciding the excitement was over, stayed outside and began nosing among the bushes.

Travis came in and moved to the middle of the room where most of the furniture had been pushed. He looked around critically. The atmosphere of the place seemed suddenly changed, charged with an electricity that had not been there before.

"I like it," he said, nodding at the new color. He glanced upward. "But what about the ceiling? Saving that for last?"

Casey caught her lower lip in her teeth. "That should have been first, shouldn't it? It was just that I couldn't wait to see what the color would look like on the walls."

"That's okay. Do you have the white paint? I'll do it."

"Yes . . . oh, yes, I bought white. But really, I don't want you to . . . I mean, there's no reason you should—"

"And how about another roller?"

She hesitated. "Well, yes, I bought two of them. I mean, if you're sure—"

"That's what I came for."

"All right, here." She went to the corner where she'd put her paint supplies and produced the second roller.

He leaned close to her to pick up the can of paint, and she could feel the heat from his body, see the way one strand of his dark hair curled over his ear as he poured paint into a tray.

He turned unexpectedly toward her. "I've missed you," he said, giving her a quick kiss that took Casey's breath away and left her knees weak. But before she could react further, he reached up and started rolling paint onto the ceiling. He was tall enough not to need the ladder.

For a moment she watched him. Then, with a quick mental shake, she climbed the ladder herself and used her brush to fill in the spaces near the top of the wall where her roller hadn't reached. She had to make an effort to keep her hand steady. For several minutes they both worked quietly, although Casey was aware of Travis humming under his breath as he stroked the paint on.

"Is Michael still doing well?" she asked at last, casting about frantically for a safe subject.

"Better than I'd have dreamed a week ago. I hope to get a few of those tubes out of him soon, and once I do, we can begin to think about letting him go home."

"That's wonderful." Casey concentrated on finishing a high corner. "I'm going to put an ad in the paper," she said. "For the cottage. I think it's perfect for a couple, and I'd feel a lot better knowing there was someone here right near Constance."

"When you go back to Washington, you mean."

"Well...yes." She could feel the wild thumping of her heart.

The cottage was silent for a few moments except for the swishing strokes of brush and roller. Then Travis said thoughtfully, "You know, I always did wonder about your coming up here in June. Why would a Washington society photographer pick that month to run away when it's got to be the biggest wedding month of the year?''

"Run away!" Casey exclaimed indignantly. "I wasn't running away!" She twisted on the ladder to look at him.

He shrugged. "Nothing to be ashamed of. I suppose everybody does it now and then. I certainly have."

She studied him briefly, then turned back to the wall.

"Well, I suppose . . . maybe I was, sort of. I told myself I did it because my father was so anxious for me to help Constance out."

"But that wasn't the real reason?"

"I didn't say that. That was part of the reason. My father is a pretty high-pressure kind of man." Behind her she could hear the even strokes of the roller.

"What was the rest of the reason?"

Casey hesitated, brush in hand. She'd never admitted, even to herself, what had made her decide to come here. Was it only her father's insistence? She tried to remember. Or was it the longing to be off somewhere new, somewhere by herself, to move away from a life she'd come to regard as increasingly trivial and monotonous? But all that had changed now, hadn't it? She thought of the museum show, and once more warring emotions jangled through her body.

"I'm not sure," she said.

"And you don't really feel as much of an outsider now, do you?" he asked softly.

Still holding the brush, she turned to him. "I guess I shouldn't have said that," she admitted. "But, yes, I'm beginning to feel more . . . accepted. I mean, by my aunt," she added hastily. "Constance calls me by my name now, you know. At last. I think she's actually begun to like me.'' She went on painting with small, swift strokes, but she was only too aware of his silence behind her.

"Constance isn't the only one," he said at last in a low voice. She heard him put down his roller and tray, heard his measured steps as he walked across the room, threading his way through the shrouded furniture. Slowly she turned and saw that he stood just below her, looking up.

"Well, I'm glad of that, of course," she said weakly. "I mean, it's nice to be..."

He took the brush from her hand and set it down, then put both hands on her waist and gently lifted her to the floor. His arms went around her and he bent his head, his lips seeking hers.

Excitement raced through Casey's veins and tingled along her arms as she felt the pressure of his mouth on hers, sensual and insistent, felt herself responding as if she'd been waiting for this moment her whole life. All her good resolutions about staying aloof and not getting entangled seemed to fly away....

He pulled back, gazing down at her tenderly.

"You're an incredible woman, Casey Logan."

"No, I'm not. Not at all. I'm just—" Her words were cut off as he kissed her again, a deeper, longer kiss, and pulled her tight against the length of his own body. Casey struggled to retain control of herself, but her thoughts kept dissolving, washing away like sand under an incoming wave as his hand moved up and down her back, pressing her closer. Her own hands were caressing the back of his head where the hair grew thick and curled a little. And then, surprising herself, she was holding him tightly, too, letting her body fit pliantly against his harder, more muscular one. The world and its concerns lay outside, far away from either of them, and Casey felt herself being swept along, caught up in a surge of emotional surrender. Suddenly she pulled away, not trusting her own strength, her own will to handle the situation. How would she ever sort out her feelings for this man?

"Look," she whispered, "this isn't a good idea. I mean, in two weeks I'm returning to Washington. I'm not ready for any permanent attachments at this point in my life." She felt she was expressing herself awkwardly, that what she'd said was not really what she meant.

He was silent, and at last she looked up at him. By the harsh overhead light she could see his shadowed eyes, no longer warm but cool and enigmatic, as if he was assessing her. It was only for a moment, then it was gone, to be replaced by a dispassionate smile.

"Don't worry, I wasn't planning on a permanent arrangement," he said lightly. "As a matter of fact, I've had about enough of girls with influential fathers."

Casey felt stung; his blow had landed in a vulnerable spot. She tried to keep her voice level. "Your life is here. This town, all your interests. That health-care facility you talked about setting up. It's just that I don't think it would be—"

"You really had me fooled," he cut in, his tone wry. "I thought for a while that those interests you mentioned were your interests, too. But this was just your good deed, wasn't it? Your family obligation? When you go back to Washington, it'll be forgotten, right?"

"It isn't like that at all," she protested, but he turned away.

"Well, if you're leaving in two weeks, we'd better not waste any more time on unimportant stuff. Let's get this job done." He picked up the roller and began moving it over the ceiling again with long, swift strokes. Casey watched him, feeling a stab of regret, a pain around her heart, which pulsed with a heavy, measured beat.

SHE PAINTED and scrubbed the cottage all during the following week, wearing herself out every day as she tried to dull her painful emotions. Leo Bates mended the roof. Then, admiring her work inside, he insisted it would be a shame not to have the place look as good on the outside.

"I'll just pick up some exterior paint and slap it on," he said. Casey protested, but Leo was determined, and he began to work methodically at the little building, pipe clenched between his teeth. In no time he had the clapboards covered with fresh, sparkling white. His wife, Anna, appeared one day and bore away with her all the cushions and chair seats that needed restoring from the ravages of mice and time. "We'll work on them at our next Friday get-together," she said.

The pets feature in the semi-weekly *Barker Springs News Leader* brought results almost at once. A family with two children came to select a dog and left with two. "Well, you can see, they just belong together," Constance told them, although she went indoors later and blew her nose loudly, and Casey suspected each adoption would be a sorrow to her. But she'd made no objection when Casey had suggested the arrangement with the newspaper and protested that she was delighted to have the animals go to good homes. With the next edition of the paper two more dogs and a cat were adopted.

Fretting about her enforced idleness, Constance insisted on setting out the impatiens herself, and she managed to do it, sitting on an old blanket and digging away in the border next to the house. The front lawn was free of clutter now, the scruffy truck parked discreetly in the rear, the fence mended, the grass mowed. The sheriff hadn't found the culprits of the vandalism of the previous week, but the road had been quiet, the nights undisturbed, and there was no sign of a recurrence.

Sitting at the kitchen table Thursday evening, Casey worked at composing an ad for the paper. "What do you think sounds better, Constance? 'Rural setting, on quiet road,' or 'convenient to all transportation'?"

"Lord, I don't know." Constance, across the table from her, furrowed her brow in thought. "Maybe you'd better put both."

"Yes, maybe." Casey bit the end of her pencil, unaware of the long, scrutinizing look her aunt was giving her.

"My stars, Casey," Constance said quietly. "How different everything is since you came here. This time just a month ago I was sitting in that big old chair feeling sorry for myself and wondering how I was ever going to make ends meet, and now it seems as if things just might work out."

"Of course they will," Casey said firmly. "And I'm sure they would have even if I hadn't been here."

"No. Everybody needs help sometimes, and I was just too mule-headed stubborn to accept it. I surely will miss you when you go back."

Casey darted a quick look at her aunt. She had said nothing to her about the phone call from Harrison Bentley a few days ago. He'd officially offered her the museum-show job, which started in two weeks.

Constance gave her a one-sided smile. "Well, you are planning to leave soon, aren't you?"

Casey sighed. "There's an important assignment waiting for me back in Washington."

"I'm not surprised. And I don't want to keep you here fussing over my affairs. You've done wonders as it is."

Casey was touched by her aunt's faith in her, but fearful, when she reflected on it, that Constance might be expecting more than she could deliver.

With the work on the cottage proceeding well, Casey decided to clean up around the outside, and she set to work hacking the tangled underbrush and the young saplings that had sprung up. She loaded them onto Constance's big-wheeled garden cart and brought them back to burn, when Constance let out a cry. "Don't burn them! The beavers can use them."

So Casey pushed the cart across the meadow to the little stand of woods and the beaver pond. Constance had identified some of the saplings as aspen—apparently a beaver favorite. All the way there Casey thought about the evening she and Travis had watched the little family of beavers swimming and playing in the pond. The kits would be growing rapidly; she wouldn't be here to see them when they reached adulthood.

She was surprised to feel such a sharp stab of regret.

CHAPTER EIGHT

PETE RIDLEY HIMSELF delivered Casey's little red car, restored and shining, and Casey spent long moments circling it and admiring the workmanship.

"Now that's new, that bumper," Pete pointed out. "But the bodywork here—and here on the fender—my son did that. Couldn't tell, could you, where the damage was?"

"Not in a million years," Casey agreed. He insisted on going over the bill with her, explaining every item, then she wrote him a check, assuring him that the insurance company was taking care of it.

"Don't forget the wedding this weekend," he reminded her as his son drove up in the truck to take him back to town. Casey nodded and waved them off, promising to be there with her camera.

"Mercy!" Constance said admiringly from the porch as Casey returned. "That's the prettiest little thing I ever saw. I'd a good deal rather ride in that than in the truck to go to the hospital."

"Hospital?" Casey's head came up. Constance's face was alive with suppressed excitement and her dark eyes were snapping.

"Tomorrow morning. Travis wants us to meet him there. He just called to say he's got that Dr. Somers visiting him. Travis will be taking him to see Michael in the morning, and if we're there too, they'll X-ray my leg and maybe I can get rid of this cast. Lord, will I be glad of that!''

Casey swallowed uncomfortably and forced a smile. The prospect of seeing Travis again gave her an anxious, uncertain feeling. And Dr. Somers—that was the doctor who wanted Travis to come work with him in New England. Did this visit mean Travis had decided to leave Barker Springs, after all? She decided not to spoil her aunt's delight by mentioning the possibility.

"He said to bring the other shoe," Constance said delightedly.

"Other shoe?"

"Yes, you know, if the cast comes off, I might be able to walk again."

"Oh, Constance, I do hope so," Casey said. She felt vaguely disloyal for the thought she had—that if Constance were whole and able to walk again, she herself would feel less guilty about leaving.

That afternoon she gave the car a test drive, taking it into town and enjoying the soft ride, the purr of the engine. After the bone-shaking rattle of Constance's old pickup it was sheer luxury. Was this her first step back toward the life she'd known before Barker Springs? Casey considered the matter wryly and wondered if anything would ever be quite the same again. She kept her eyes firmly on the road and didn't look at Travis Grant's house as she drove by.

She stopped in front of the newspaper office and went inside with the ad she and Constance had composed. The woman at the front desk counted the words and Casey paid in advance. Then Joan Singleton, hearing their voices, came over from her desk and joined them. She and Casey discussed the success of the pet-adoption column, and Casey handed her two new pictures.

"I never thought about it when you were here before, Casey," the editor said, "but you mentioned not having a place to develop your film. We have a small darkroom here. Only good for black-and-white, of course. Color stuff would still have to be sent out of town. But you're welcome to use it."

"Could I really?" Casey was delighted. "Oh, I'd appreciate that so much. As a matter of fact there is something I've been hanging on to until I could get back to my own darkroom. But if it would really be all right..."

"Any time," Joan said. "I hear you're the official photographer for the Ridley wedding this weekend. We'll use a picture of that, too."

"Good. I'll see you get it," Casey said, waving as she left.

SHE HAD STEELED HERSELF against reacting the next time she saw Travis. It would be easy to stay in control in the hospital's impersonal atmosphere, she told herself, especially with a stranger present in the person of Dr. Somers. But Dr. Somers himself, tall and distinguished-looking with an attractive head of gray hair and full gray mustache, tossed the whole scene into chaos when he held out his hand to her and spoke for the first time.

"So *you're* Casey Logan. I might have known you'd look like this. And you must be the reason I'm having so much trouble trying to persuade this fellow he's needed in New Hampshire."

Casey stood there speechless and blushing in the hospital's reception room as the doctor pumped her hand enthusiastically; in the background, Travis looked acutely uncomfortable.

Constance, never ill at ease, said in her forthright way, "Well, if you keep on trying to coax our doctor away, I'm not at all sure I'm going to like you."

Dr. Somers flashed her a winning smile. "That would be a great disappointment to me, Mrs. Pritchard. But not to worry. He's already said no to my offer."

Casey glanced up in surprise, her eyes seeking out Travis's. For a moment their looks collided, but his was unreadable—cool and distant.

"No, he's got me here on another pretext," Dr. Somers went on. "Wants me to discuss a new project he's got in mind. A health-care facility for this town— what's its name again?"

"Barker Springs," Casey supplied.

"That's it. Well, he thinks that's what the place needs, so we're doing some conferring on it. I'll tell you one thing—you've got a doctor here a lot of big hospitals would be glad to get hold of. I was telling him just this morning—"

"All right, all right," Travis put in smoothly. "Let's stick to the business at hand. And first of all, let's take Constance to radiology and X-ray that leg. Then Dr. Somers and I can decide whether the cast comes off."

Dr. Somers looked heavenward. "As if my opinion's needed. I'd trust this fellow with my *own* broken leg, for heaven's sake. All right, all right. Come along, Mrs. Pritchard."

She gave him an arch smile. "Constance would be fine," she said.

Casey said she'd wait for them. She had no wish to be in close proximity to Travis Grant any more than was absolutely necessary. So she read old magazines and drank coffee while they were gone. On a sudden inspiration, she took out the camera she always carried with her, so that when the trio returned, with Constance cast-free and jubilantly leaning on an aluminum cane, Casey was ready to record the moment.

"An absolutely splendid recovery," Dr. Somers pronounced. "All she has to do now is behave prudently and not overdo. Young lady, you'll have to watch her."

"I'll do my best," Casey promised.

"And don't forget the party, Leland," Constance said through the open window of the car as they prepared to leave.

Dr. Somers smiled, bending over to speak to her. "I'm looking forward to it. This is shaping up into a much better holiday than I'd anticipated."

As she started the car, Casey glanced out her side and unexpectedly met Travis's eyes. He said nothing, but took a backward step and lifted one hand in farewell. Casey felt a turning-over of her heart, a sudden lonely feeling as if all her days in Barker Springs were rushing toward an end, rolling up behind her like a carpet. She backed up and drove out of the hospital parking lot, then forced her attention to the present. When she looked at her aunt, she was startled to find Constance eyeing her closely. Before the older woman could speak, Casey said quickly, "Leland? You're on first-name terms already? And what's this about a party?"

Constance waved her hand in an expansive gesture. "Oh, goodness, I never believe in formality. Besides, I liked him. The party's in honor of Michael. He's coming home tomorrow—just found out for sure. I went by his room and talked to Shirley. Of course he won't be able to do anything but lie on the couch, so it'll be a pretty quiet party, but we'll celebrate just the same. Leland thought it was a great idea."

Now it was Casey's turn to give her aunt a close look. "You don't say," she murmured.

"Yes. I told him about you, about your work and how you're going back to Washington soon. You haven't said much about it, but the little I've heard sounds quite exciting," Constance added thoughtfully.

"Why don't you come to Washington and see the exhibition?" Casey suggested, swinging the car onto the narrow county road to her aunt's house.

"Oh, I don't know." Her aunt frowned, considering it. "Washington, the circles my brother travels in—it's not exactly my style. Besides, I was figuring when you came back here you could tell me all about it."

"What makes you think I'll be back?" Casey said teasingly.

Constance threw her a withering look. "Oh, for heaven's sake, girl, of course you'll be back. You've got one foot in the place now."

Casey felt a sudden mistiness in her eyes and blinked rapidly. Somehow her aunt's brusque assumption that she belonged was the hardest of all to take, when Casey herself knew so well that she didn't.

THE FESTIVITIES honoring Michael's homecoming were much too low-key to be called a real party. Neighbors and friends from the village were in and out of the Townsend's place all afternoon, bringing food and flowers from their gardens, making the little house bloom with color and setting Shirley and Michael up with meals for the coming week. Some of the good wishes spilled over onto Constance, whose appearance without crutches surprised them all. Dr. Somers supervised the making of a fruit punch, then mingled with the visitors, paying special attention to Constance. Lee Nelson arrived bearing a tape of a new rap group, which Shirley implored her son not to play until later. Michael, looking pale and thin but with happiness sparkling in his eyes, lay on the couch until Travis decided he needed to sleep and helped him into his bedroom for a nap.

Lee sought out Casey and complimented her on all she'd done for her aunt.

"The place looks absolutely great, Casey," she said. "I wouldn't have believed anybody could make so much difference in such a short time." Lee's dark hair fell forward around her face in two soft curves. Her blue jacket, loose and square, was worn over a short, white linen dress, and a heavy gold bracelet circled her wrist. She looked so elegantly stylish that Casey almost had to smile. She, Casey, was the big-city girl, who should, by rights, have brought big-city style to the country, but almost since her first day here she'd worn work clothes. Even today she was dressed in the simplest blue cotton skirt and T-shirt.

"I had a great time doing it," Casey admitted.

"Well, we all think it's wonderful," Lee said. Her eyes moved away from Casey for a moment, and Casey saw that they were following Travis as he came out of Michael's bedroom and went to speak to Dr. Somers. She immediately returned her attention to Casey. "Now what about this cottage? Are you looking for a tenant?"

Casey explained that she was putting an ad in the paper. "But if it doesn't bring results I may call on you to see if you can find us one."

"Great. Just let me know. Anything I can do to help."

They chatted for a few more minutes, and then Lee excused herself and hurried across the room, stopping to speak to Shirley en route but managing to wind up beside Travis. Casey watched them talking together for a moment, then suddenly turned away, feeling teary and uncertain and strongly suspecting that all her emotions were written plainly on her face. She slipped out of the house and crossed the road to Constance's. Why was she finding it so difficult to handle this situation? She'd been attracted to Travis, it was true; perhaps he had even been attracted to her. But that wasn't love, was it? And he'd made it quite clear that he'd had a bad experience before and was in no way anxious to rush into another commitment. She had a wonderfully exciting assignment ahead of her in Washington, something she would have been delirious about only a few weeks ago. Why was she feeling such an emptiness as the time for leaving grew nearer? And why, when she closed her eyes even for an instant, did she always see the same picture behind her lids—the image of a lean face, impossibly blue eyes and soft hair falling forward?

The afternoon had disappeared without her realizing it. Now all the shadows were long and blue as she made her way up the front walk. She paused at the foot of the porch steps, and then on an impulse circled the house and walked through the backyard, out past the kennels and the barn, across the meadow toward the beaver pond. Everything was quiet, with no sign of the inhabitants. Casey went up onto the dam and sat quietly, listening to the meadow sounds around her—the whirr of insects, bird song, the occasional scurrying of some small creature in the tall grass. *I'm going to miss this place,* she thought.

How surprising, she reflected, that in such a short time she should have found herself involved with so many new people, new situations, and that all of them should matter so much to her. Michael's homecoming. The

Ridley girl's wedding on Saturday. Constance's recovery. The work on the cottage. Carefully Casey kept her thoughts away from the one person who had come to matter most.

She sighed and glanced at the small pile of saplings and brush she'd carried out here from the cottage. It had been considerably depleted, all the tender twigs gone and much of the bark peeled off.

"Are you the one who brought that out here for them?"

Casey looked up quickly, startled to see Travis standing on the shore. She swallowed and said in a light, teasing voice, "You must be the original deer stalker or tracker or whatever it is. I never hear you creeping up on me."

"Not exactly creeping." He smiled. "You were lost in thought."

She nodded toward the pile of saplings. "I brought those out here the other day. The beavers seem to have approved of them."

"More than approved, I'd say. Looks as if they had a feast. You've got some aspen in there, I think. That's a favorite food with beavers, although they'll eat whatever's available. Of course if it was later in the season, they'd have carried it underwater and stashed it away for winter." He came over and dropped down casually beside her.

His nearness sent a frisson of excitement running along Casey's arms. She tried to keep a tight grip on herself—the unconcerned manner, the unflustered voice.

"I'll bet that's something *you* don't approve of," she said with a small, tight smile. "Feeding animals in the wild."

"True, I don't." His own smile was tentative. "I mean, as a matter of principle I don't. It's best if they make their own way, and Mother Nature weeds out the ones not equipped to survive. She maintains the balance better than we could. Only the way things are, I guess that little bit you brought won't do any harm."

"What do you mean, 'the way things are'?" Everything he said challenged and interested her, even when she tried to remain distant.

"Oh, you know, their habitat being invaded by developers. Fast cars on roads. Trappers. Their food supply being bulldozed away. So maybe we do owe them a little something in the way of help and can forget about principles for once."

Casey nodded. "Do they really store their winter food supply under the water? Why not along the shore?"

"Because they spend the winter in their lodge." He gestured toward it. "This whole pond'll be iced over. They'll use their underwater doorway to get to their food supply, but they won't come out."

Casey glanced at him curiously, then remembered a poised, stylish Lee Nelson looking up at him and talking earnestly.

She moved a few inches away from him. "How did you think Michael was doing?" she asked in a quick change of subject.

If he noticed her subtle movement he didn't show it. "I'm pleased," he said thoughtfully. "I'm more than pleased. I'm astonished. So's Leland. That strain of meningitis is a particularly virulent one—it can have really bad consequences. But he seems to have come through it remarkably well. It may put his college plans on hold for a while, but he says that doesn't bother him.

Says he's giving some thought to going in a new direction, anyway. He might study medicine.''

"Really!" she exclaimed in surprise. "That's quite a lot to take on. I mean, his mother must have a hard time managing as it is."

"Oh, there's always a way. Look—there they are." He pointed across the pond, and Casey saw the now familiar furry noses cleaving the water, V-shaped trails behind them.

"Mr. and Mrs.," she whispered, identifying them. "What about the kids?"

"There, following right along."

All four headed toward the pile of saplings, and Casey and Travis watched in silence as the beavers pulled themselves out of the water, up onto the bank and settled in to strip bark from the slender logs. They worked methodically, but with obvious enjoyment, the only altercation occurring when the two kits seized the same stick. Small angry grunts could be heard as they pulled the stick in two directions until finally one of the kits fell backward into the water. The little animal scrambled out quickly but this time found itself another branch to work on. When they were full, the kits returned to the water and began their usual games of tag, and a new one Casey hadn't seen before—rushing at each other and then diving underwater just as they were about to collide.

"They're growing," she murmured softly.

"Yes. They'll be big enough to help store winter food later in the season."

At the sound of their voices, the adult beavers stopped eating and turned warily in their direction. Casey and Travis remained motionless while they were inspected as possible sources of danger, but the two beavers apparently decided they were safe.

"They're coming to know us," Travis whispered.

"Oh, how wonderful!" Casey felt a genuine thrill.

"Wonderful, but dangerous. I'd feel better if they didn't trust too many people."

For several more minutes they sat quietly, observing the adult beavers on the bank. The parents had finished eating and now sat quietly side by side, occasionally glancing out at the frolicking kits. Then, on the still night air, came a series of small sounds, almost like voices.

"Are they talking to each other?" Casey whispered.

"In a way, I suppose."

Straining her eyes in the dusk to watch the pair of animals, Casey saw them leaning toward each other, their two faces touching, nuzzling softly.

Travis reached for her hand, pointing with his other one. She nodded, watching breathlessly, feeling a tingle of excitement. But only part of that excitement came from the thrill of witnessing this intimate moment. The other part came from the strong, warm hand that had closed over hers.

They stayed until the darkness was almost complete and the beavers had returned to their lodge. Then they got up to begin walking back toward the house. He didn't reach for her hand again and she made sure there was a careful space between them. They could see across the meadow to the other side of the road; most of the cars had left the Townsend house.

"I apologize for acting the way I did the other night in the cottage," he said at last. Casey said nothing as they went on walking through the tall, sweet grass. "I thought . . . that I'd gotten over what happened in California, but I guess it's still a sore spot. I shouldn't have lashed out at you that way. And I should have asked you about the assignment you have to get back to Washington for."

Casey glanced up at him and saw that he was looking at her, his face shadowed and softened by night.

"It's an exhibition," she said. "Of young American photographers and their work. But with special emphasis on portraiture. Faces of America, it's called. And I'm to help judge it and be in charge of making selections, doing the hanging and so on."

"That sounds great. And very important."

"Well, it's the kind of thing I've been wanting to do. It'll make a nice change from kiddie parties and graduation pictures."

"Then I'm glad for you."

They walked on in silence for a time, until Casey said, "I'll miss this place."

She could hear laughter in his voice. "Weed pulling, fence mending, painting, the occasional bit of carpentry. I can see how you'd miss all that."

"You still seem to feel I'm just up here amusing myself for a while," she said sharply.

"No, on the contrary, I was complimenting you."

Casey took a deep breath, wondering why she reacted so passionately to everything he said, why she was so quick to take offense. "Sorry," she murmured.

As they came alongside the old barn, Casey suddenly smelled smoke. "Hey, what's burning?"

"I smell it, too." He dashed to the barn door and poked his head inside. "Nothing wrong here. What about the house?" Both of them ran toward it, flinging doors open and looking everywhere.

"Could it be someone just burning trash?" Casey wondered, breathless, as they paused on the back porch.

"No—wait a minute," she said a moment later. "The cottage!"

They left the house and ran for the cottage, stumbling along the narrow path in the darkness. Travis's long legs covered the distance rapidly.

"It's here!" he yelled, and Casey, a few yards behind him, smelled the thickening smoke. "Open the door so we can get some water!"

Casey fumbled for the key and had the door open in an instant. She turned on the lights and dashed to the kitchen sink where she filled a bucket with water. When she carried it outside she found Travis kicking away a small smoldering pile that had been shoved up against the house. He grabbed the bucket from her and doused the whole mess, causing steam and acrid black smoke to billow up. Casey ran back for more water, and they continued drenching the pile until there were no sparks left.

"How could that have happened?" Casey demanded. "I'm sure I didn't leave any debris lying around." She was breathing hard, her cheeks red with exertion. Travis's white shirt was smudged with soot and his hair tumbled over his forehead. "Oh, Travis, look at the mess!" Without thinking, she leaned against him, regarding with dismay the long streaks of black smeared across the snowy white wall Leo Bates had just finished painting. Travis's arm came around her, holding her close.

"Oh, it isn't that bad," he said comfortingly. "Leo can have that fixed up in half an hour." He bent to kiss her cheek lightly, and in spite of the tumult of the moment, Casey felt a churning deep inside. It was a response that clicked on with all the immediacy of a light bulb. She edged carefully away from him.

"But how did it happen?" she asked in a despairing voice. "Leo and I have both taken such care to keep the place cleaned up. We'd never have..." She paused, horrified. "Those two!" she exclaimed. "Those bikers. They've been around here again."

"I didn't hear them," he said, his voice thoughtful.

"No, neither did I—but we were all talking in Shirley's house. We wouldn't have noticed, would we?"

"Perhaps not. Well, look, it's not serious. Nothing's been damaged, really, and Leo will fix up the smudges."

"That's not the point. What scares me is the idea that these hoodlums are tearing through the countryside doing things like this. What do you do about such random violence? How do you fight it?" He said nothing, and she went on, angrier and angrier. "It's taken me all this time to restore some optimism to Constance. She was just about ready to give up when I came here. I mean, she said she wasn't, and she was hanging on to that feisty defiance of hers, but I knew she couldn't hold out very long. But lately she's been like a different person, talking about the future and making plans. Even when the place was vandalized—I mean, it was just malicious mischief—but a fire is more serious. What's going to happen when she hears about this?"

"Hears about what?" asked a loud, husky voice behind them. Travis and Casey turned to see Constance, leaning on her new cane and supported on the other side by Dr. Somers. The yellow dog, Sarge, and the little black one, Nick, tagged after them.

"Oh, Constance, you shouldn't have walked out here," Casey wailed.

"Just what I said," Leland Somers put in. "Walking on a wooded path in the dark is not what the doctor ordered for a convalescent. She paid no attention whatever. Smelled smoke, she said. What's going on?''

"Somebody...started a fire," Casey said reluctantly.

"What is it, those two on the bikes again?" Constance demanded.

"I suppose so," Casey murmured. "Of course it is! Who else would do such a destructive thing?"

In the light from the open cottage door, Casey could see her aunt's face change from anxious to angry. "Well, if that Hank Beltzer thinks he's getting another vote for sheriff out of me he'd better think again," Constance said. "If he can't do any better than he's done so far, I might consider running myself. Come on, Leland, let's go in and call him. I wish it was later so I could get him out of bed." They began making their careful way back to the house. Old Sarge plodded along behind them, but Nick lingered by the cottage, sniffing at the pile of debris and stepping gingerly over the muddy ground.

"There, you see?" Travis said. "She took it very well. I think it's going to take more than one small fire to get Constance down."

Casey gazed into his face. "What if there's more?" she whispered. "What if I'm not here and something really bad happens?"

"No point in worrying about it any more tonight," he said. "Come on. Let's close the place up and get back."

But Casey was suddenly unable to move. She stood beside him feeling cold and frightened, and her whole body began to tremble.

"I just don't know how..." she began, but didn't finish.

"Wait a minute here." He put an arm around her shoulders and looked deep into her eyes. "Hey, you really do care about all this, don't you? Come on inside. You'd better sit down for a bit." Gently he steered her through the open cottage door. "Is anything working here? Stove in order? How about tea?"

She nodded weakly. "Leo and I have been making it when we worked. It's on the counter." She nodded toward the kitchen end of the cottage, and he urged her into a chair and went to fix the tea. She sat there, motionless, feeling spent and confused. It was all too much, she thought, closing her eyes wearily. Too much was happening to her lately. Too many emotions crowding into a life that had known only routine and regularity.

He returned with a damp washcloth and wiped the smudges off her face and hands. She looked up into his face as he did so, then managed a smile. "You don't look so great yourself," she said, and took the cloth from him, wiping soot from his nose and chin. He smiled back at her and went for the tea. She drank it obediently, leaning back in the chair and feeling stronger with every sip.

"I wonder who'll be living here—once it's rented, I mean," she said softly.

"Whoever they are, they'll be lucky. You've made it into a great place."

"It's nice, isn't it?" She glanced around, taking in the clean, painted walls of soft green, the old furniture brushed and polished back into life, the worn rug with its mellow, muted colors. "It needs a few things yet. Some curtains, and maybe a clock for the mantel, but even the way it is I love it."

He had sunk down beside her on the floor. Now he reached up to take her cup, and all in one motion got up and pulled her with him, pressing her close, finding her lips with his own.

"Casey," he murmured in her ear. "Casey, darling, I don't think we've read each other right ever since we met."

Casey, not trusting herself to speak, shook her head against the hollow of his neck.

"This is what I've wanted all along," he whispered, "only it never seemed to be right—something was always in the way. Mostly my thickheadedness."

"Or mine," she whispered back, raising her face to his again.

This time his kiss enveloped her hungrily, and Casey kissed him back, responding, letting the wonder of the moment consume her. She knew she'd never belonged anywhere as much as she belonged here—in this small house in the woods, in the arms of this man who was still an enigma to her. It was the essential rightness of it that washed over her now, as clear and cool and transparent as water in a country brook. She felt a sudden assurance, a confidence, that this was her future. This was what fate had in store for her. She and Travis would find their way, would live their lives together. Tonight was the beginning. Why had she wasted so much time worrying about it? It all seemed so simple, so inevitable now. Hazily, as in a dream, she felt herself being lifted in his arms and carried into the bedroom, dimly lit by the light from the main room. But tonight she saw none of the things that delighted her by day—the little pine chest, the cherrywood table, the small, ladder-back chair. Tonight she was aware only of the four-poster bed with its patchwork quilt, and of the strong arms that lowered her onto it. And for this moment, for this one night, it became her home.

CHAPTER NINE

HE WAS GONE when she woke up, but she was snugly covered with the patchwork quilt. Through the window she could see that it wasn't daylight yet, but some gray was starting to appear in the sky, and a few birds had begun to sing busily, as if to remind the sleeping world that it was high time to be awake. Casey allowed herself a moment's blissful remembrance in her warm cocoon of quilt, reliving the passion of the night before. But passion—that had only been part of it, she reflected. Permanence, belonging to someone, a future she could picture for the first time, with the two of them planning and sharing—that was an even greater magic. Reluctantly she pushed back the covers and located her clothes, dressing hastily and smoothing the bed. She took a last look around at the cottage, feeling a fullness of joy that caused her throat to tighten. Then she opened the door. Nick was asleep on the doorstep, his black coat spangled with pearly dew.

"Come on, Nick," she murmured, leaning down to touch him. He roused himself with a huge yawn and together they made their way back along the path toward the house.

Everything was quiet inside, and Casey noticed her aunt had rather pointedly left the screen door unlatched for her. She bathed and dressed quickly, brushing out her hair and fastening it back in its single braid. She went downstairs again and made coffee before feeding Nick and Sarge and then heading out to the kennels to take care of the other dogs. She fed goat pellets to Belle and saw that Walter had a fresh supply of branches to work on. When she returned to the house, Constance was downstairs wearing a voluminous Oriental-looking housecoat and drinking coffee.

"Well!" she said with a smile. "That was quite a day, wasn't it?"

Casey, who had half expected dismay over the fire or disapproval over her own all-night absence, decided that Constance Pritchard was not an easy woman to figure out.

"You might say that," she agreed. "What about the sheriff?"

"Said he'd be out here this morning to look around. Fat lot of good that's going to do. He knows as much about fighting crime as I do. Less, if you come right down to it. I watch Perry Mason, at least."

"How does the leg feel? I hope you're not overdoing this," Casey said severely.

"Feels wonderful. Leland's stopping by later to take me out riding. He wants to see some of the country around here."

Settling down at the table with her own coffee, Casey glanced at her aunt. "A date?" she asked, raising her eyebrows.

"Well, yes. A date. You young people don't have a corner on that sort of thing, you know."

Casey, feeling she had a corner on the whole world this morning, refrained from saying so. "You're going to miss him when he goes back to New Hampshire. I never saw two people hit it off so well."

Constance waved this away with one of her grand gestures of dismissal. "Good heavens, this is the 1990s, dear. Travel's not a problem. He came here once—he can come again. Or . . . I might go there, if I feel like it."

"Is it that serious?" Casey stared.

"It's not serious at all," Constance said. "It's fun. If it gets serious, you'll be the first to know."

Casey suspected her aunt was teasing, and she grew serious herself for a moment, trying not to think of the many obstacles between her and Travis. Distance, divergent careers, worlds-apart backgrounds. But the memory of his arms around her, his body next to hers in the night, overrode all other considerations. Constance seemed to read her thoughts.

"Some things are just meant to be, and others aren't," she said flatly. "I always feel if it's meant to be, if it's right, it'll work out. Of course, it doesn't hurt sometimes to give the thing a little push." She gave her niece a knowing look, then glanced outside. "There's the sheriff. You go see him, will you, dear? I've got to get dressed."

Hank Beltzer was earnest and polite and obviously completely baffled. He studied the area beside the cottage, kicked at the ashes, then shook his head worriedly.

"Beats me," he said, squinting into the sunlight. "It sure does. Why would anybody do such a thing?"

Casey couldn't help feeling a little sorry for him as she watched him poking through the debris, peering diligently through his wraparound sunglasses. Barker Springs was no high-crime area. Probably he never had anything more serious to cope with than an occasional speeder or a cat up a tree.

"Kids, you know, they do get up to devilment now and then. Don't realize it could amount to something serious," he said. She thought he was trying to convince himself as much as her.

Tentatively Casey mentioned the bikers who'd been in the area lately, and he nodded and said he was following up that lead. He added that he'd keep an eye on the house. He and his deputy would patrol the road faithfully, he promised. Casey thanked him and saw him off, not at all reassured.

Still, the morning was bright and promising, and she was feeling a cloud-nine euphoria whenever she let her thoughts drift to Travis. She would keep herself busy, that was the best thing. She had a dozen matters she could see to. She would go to the newspaper office and develop the film she'd been saving. That would take some time. Then she'd buy groceries. And she'd stop at the Townsends' across the road to see how Michael was and what she could do to help the two of them. Shirley was still not back at work, anxious about Michael and his care. Maybe if Casey stayed with him for an hour or two Shirley could get away long enough for a new hairdo or a trip to the library.

Planning her day, filling up the hours ahead, Casey knew that what she was really doing was making time pass until she could see Travis again.

She found the newspaper office in its usual state of casual disarray, with word processors humming, and people scurrying about. The woman at the front desk, whose name Casey had learned was Sandy Brenner, was on the telephone taking an ad. She waved and smiled at Casey and covered the mouthpiece to whisper, "Joan and Ed are fixing the hinge. You can go on back there."

Casey gave her a puzzled look, but followed Sandy's wave and made her way toward the rear of the office. A back door, hanging crookedly, was being worked on by the Singletons. Both of them smiled as they greeted her.

"Routine home improvement?" Casey asked.

"Mmm. Just about the usual around here," Joan said, her pleasant face looking mildly exasperated. Her reading glasses had slid farther down her nose than usual. She was holding an assortment of screws in her open palm.

Ed Singleton's hair was sticking up in unruly wisps as he bore down on a screwdriver he was using to reset an old hinge. "I should probably replace this thing. In fact, I think I will. Hang on, Joanie. I'm going to dash to the hardware store. Be right back."

Joan shook her head and grinned as he took off. She leaned over, dumping the handful of screws into an untidy toolbox on the floor. "Eddie's got about as much do-it-yourself savvy as I have, which is not much. Although I'm not bad with chewing gum and bobby pins."

"How did it happen?" Casey asked.

"Oh, it was Marv Butler. He's sober most of the time. He does odd jobs around town and he delivers papers for us. This morning we put out the new editions for him, and when he backed up his truck to load them he managed to keep right on going and pushed the door off its hinges. Don't ask me how—Marv has amazing capabilities for achieving the impossible. Especially when he's had a few, which I suspect was the case here. It's not the first time something like this has happened."

Casey nodded sympathetically. Now and then she had seen Marv, skinny, unshaven and, she suspected, unwashed, putting the paper into her aunt's mailbox.

"We're going to have to keep him out of the truck in future, that's all. He shouldn't be driving at all in my opinion, and I know for a fact he's got a bicycle. Not that he couldn't be a hazard on that, too. So, what brings you out so early?"

"I was wondering if I could take you up on that offer to use the darkroom," Casey said hesitantly. "If this isn't a good time, it's okay."

"No, gosh, it's fine," Joan insisted. "Old Marv manages to create this kind of havoc every couple of weeks. We're used to it."

"We had some havoc of our own last night," Casey said, and sketched in the incident of the fire.

Joan's brows drew together in a frown. "That's a little more serious than Marv Butler and his pickup. Kids, do you think?"

"But what kids?" Casey asked.

Joan pushed up her sliding glasses. "None that I know. And I sure don't like to think..." She let her voice trail off, shaking her head as she did so. "Well, come on. Let me show you the darkroom. That's a pretty elegant term for this cubbyhole, but it serves the purpose."

"I want to pay you," Casey insisted. "I'll be using your chemicals."

Joan waved the offer away. "You're more than welcome," she said. Joan Singleton was like the rest of the people in Barker Springs, Casey thought—warm and generous. Like all the rest except for the person—or persons—unknown who'd set that fire. The faint feeling of unease crept back over her.

But moments later in the tiny darkroom, which she suspected had been converted from a closet or large storage cupboard, she was happy and felt at home again. She concentrated on the familiar process—pouring out the developer, adding water, adding hypo, then the clearing agent, washing the film. When she'd finally finished and had hung the film to dry, she went out and found Joan, announcing that she was going to do her shopping and would come back to do the printing later.

She made her usual stops—post office, drugstore, hardware store, supermarket—picking up needed items and marveling to herself how well she'd come to know the place, how familiar all the faces looked to her now.

"Hear you're coming to the wedding tomorrow," the girl behind the drugstore counter said as Casey paid for a tube of lipstick.

"Yes, I'll be taking pictures of the event."

"No kidding! Maybe you can do that for me. I'm getting married in October," the girl bubbled.

"Maybe," Casey said, but her heart gave a small, uncertain thump. Would she really be here in October?

When she had finished her shopping she returned to the newspaper and made prints from her film. Only when she had them hung up to dry did she open the door and call Joan in to see the results.

"What do you think?" she asked. "I haven't cropped them or anything, or course."

Joan caught her breath as she looked. "Oh, Casey, they're wonderful! What are you going to do with them?"

Briefly Casey explained. The prints all showed Constance Pritchard as she sat in her old rocker on the front porch, the pile of quilting scraps in her lap, her strong-fingered hands sorting the pieces. Some showed her in profile, some in a three-quarter pose. In a few her eyes were on the work in her lap, in others they looked out over the porch railing, fixed on some distant point.

"They're terrific!" Joan said. "You're going to use only the black-and-white? Going to try for some in color?"

Casey cocked her head to one side and looked at the prints again. "Well, color adds a different dimension, but you can't beat black-and-white for dramatic effect."

"True. Are you going to tell Constance, or just hang them in the show and then let her know?"

"Haven't crossed that bridge yet." Casey grinned. She collected the prints, thanking Joan again for the use of the darkroom, and promised her pictures of the Ridley wedding. Ed Singleton was still working on the backdoor hinge as she left, and echoes of mild profanity reached her as she slipped out of the office.

Shirley Townsend was happy and flustered when Casey appeared at her door later and ordered her to take a few hours off.

"Oh, but I don't know... You've done so much for us, Casey."

"Don't be silly. I'll chat with Michael for a while and then see that he rests. You need a little time to yourself. Do some shopping or just go for a drive."

"Well, maybe I could drive into Addison Mills to the library. Dr. Grant left a list of books Michael could be reading this summer while he's resting. Did you know he's talking about studying medicine?"

"Yes, I heard."

"Of course his illness may delay things a little, but I don't care about any of that, as long as I know he's going to get better." Shirley had begun to bustle around the house, smoothing her hair, picking up her handbag. She went to the door of Michael's room and spoke to him, then returned. "I won't stay out long, Casey."

"Stay as long as you want. Please. And after you've picked out those books for Michael, pick one for yourself. Or stop in and have tea somewhere. Relax a little."

"All right." Shirley smiled self-consciously. "Maybe I will. You help yourself to anything in the kitchen, won't you? And I'm sure I'll be back before Michael needs anything. But if he should..."

Gently Casey pushed her out the door. When the car had pulled out of the drive she went inside and knocked on Michael's door. He was propped up in bed, looking bright-eyed and alert despite his new thinness. He gave her a wide grin.

"Hi, Casey. I hear you're the baby-sitter today. Come on in and tell me what's going on." He seemed more outgoing since his illness, less shy than formerly, which pleased her.

She drew a chair up beside the bed. "You wouldn't believe what's happening. Have you seen the pet-adoption column in the paper?" She went on to explain how many had been taken.

"What about Nick?" Michael asked with a hint of concern.

"Not a candidate for adoption," Casey assured him. "Nick stays."

"Good." The boy's broad grin appeared.

"Now, what about your own plans?" Casey asked.

"Well, the way I look at it," he said with enthusiasm, "all this time I've got to spend resting won't be wasted. I'll be able to do a lot of reading, and Dr. Grant says that'll help me for when I do get to enter college— I'll be better prepared."

"Oh, I'm sure it will."

"I'm anxious to get started. He's going to bring me some books of his own, and Mom's going to pick up more."

"Just don't overdo it," she said with mock sternness. "Getting well's got to be the first priority."

"That's what Travis—Dr. Grant says. He's a great guy."

Casey felt herself blushing and said quickly, "I just realized I've missed lunch. I think I'll see what's in your mom's kitchen. Anything I can get you?"

"No, I'm okay. I'm supposed to take a nap now, anyway."

Casey got up and pointed an authoritative finger at him. "Nap it is, then. But I'll be right out there if you need anything."

She made herself a peanut-butter sandwich and ate it hungrily, then brewed a pot of tea. She located Shirley's cookie jar, found it full of homemade brownies, and was about to help herself when she heard a car stop outside. She put down her cup and hurried back into the living room to look out the window. Travis had just climbed out of the Blazer and was coming up the walk.

His face showed surprise and delight when she opened the door for him, a finger to her lips. "He's taking a nap," she whispered. "I thought Shirley needed a little outing. Come into the kitchen."

"I brought him a book," Travis said, laying it on the coffee table and following her into the kitchen. "Figured he couldn't go wrong starting with *Grey's Anatomy.*" Just inside the doorway he caught her hand, spun her around and pressed her close to him, covering her mouth with a sudden kiss that took her breath away.

"I was going to stop and see you," he murmured. "But this is even better. Surprises always are."

"I was just having tea and brownies," she told him. "How does that sound?"

"Not nearly as good as what I had in mind," he groaned, then kissed her again.

"Well, tea and brownies will have to do." She grinned at him. "Come on. Sit over here." She poured tea for him, marveling at how warm and comfortable she felt with him, yet longing to touch him again, reliving in memory the pulsing urgency they had both felt the night before. "Where'd you leave Leland?"

He wrapped long fingers around his cup. "I left him hiking across the field—he wanted to see the beaver pond. I believe Constance is whipping up lemonade or something for him. Those two are certainly hitting it off."

"Are you bringing him to the wedding tomorrow?"

"I expect Constance is bringing him. But I'm planning to be there, barring any emergencies."

"She's going to miss him when he leaves. Although she's acting quite modern and philosophical about it." Casey smiled, remembering their conversation at breakfast. "How much longer will he stay?"

"Probably until Sunday morning."

Casey handed him the cookie jar, and he took a brownie. "He must be disappointed that you're not taking him up on his offer," she said.

"I guess he was at first. But I think I may be turning the tables on him."

"How?"

"He's showing a lot of interest in this health-care center I want to build. That place of his in New Hampshire is a going concern now, and he's got good people running it. It wouldn't surprise me at all if he turned up here. He likes a new challenge."

"Do you really think so? Wouldn't Constance be pleased!"

"Hey, these are good." He reached into the jar for another brownie. "One for the road." He stood up, the regret plain on his face. "Have to run if I'm going to get everything in today and free myself up for all that socializing tomorrow." He leaned over her and kissed her again. Casey's eyes closed briefly and she felt a sudden surge of happiness at the utter impossibility of this happening to her, at the total wonder of it.

SALLY RIDLEY and her mother, Tess, were in a state of fluttering excitement when Casey presented herself at their house shortly after noon the next day. Casey had, fortunately, thrown one simple blue silk dress into her suitcase. She'd hung it in the closet and not looked at it since her arrival; now she decided it was suitable for the wedding. She arrived with her photographer's bag slung over her shoulder and introduced herself, which seemed to boost the tension another notch. Both Tess Ridley and the bride blushed and stuck their hands out.

"Oh, Miss Logan, this is just so good of you," Tess said breathlessly, pushing back a wisp of hair. "Sally and I are tickled to death you're taking pictures. None of us is any hand at all at that kind of thing."

"We do appreciate it, Miss Logan," the bride said earnestly. "Won't you come have some tea or coffee?"

"No, no. Not a thing. And please call me Casey." She could see in Sally Ridley the image of her mother at the same age, both of them stocky, rosy, quick to smile. "You just go on with your preparations, and I'll get some informal shots around the house. Everything looks lovely."

The mother of the bride glanced around with concern. "Well, we're almost ready, I think. Maribelle Henderson—Bill's mother—and I've done the food between us. She's out in the kitchen right now. Maybe I'll go see if she needs any help, if you're sure you can manage."

"Please go ahead. I might just come out there and get a picture of that in a minute, if no one objects."

"Oh, my goodness. Well, no, that would be lovely. I'll be up to help you dress in two shakes, dear," she said to her daughter, then bustled off through the small, flower-filled house, patting at her hair as she went.

Casey turned to the bride. "Would it be all right, do you think, to take a few shots out there in the kitchen?"

"I'm sure they'd both love it," Sally Ridley said with a giggle, waiting while Casey got her camera ready and stepped into the kitchen. She came back in a few minutes, shaking her head in disbelief.

"Never saw so much food in my life," she murmured. "Now, what's next?" Sally, in blue jeans and untucked shirt, had sunk down on the stairs, looking bewildered and a little panicky. Casey recognized the symptoms and sat on the step below her. "This has all the appearances of a really successful wedding," she said reassuringly. "Good food and a beautiful bride. And believe me, I've photographed a lot of them."

"Really?" Sally gave her a nervous look.

"Absolutely." Casey adjusted her camera and said casually, "Tell me a little about the groom. Bill, is that his name?"

"Yes, Bill Henderson." Sally brightened visibly. "He's starting up his own trucking company, and I suppose it'll take him away a lot at first. But I teach school, you know—first grade—so I'm busy too."

Casey stood up in a leisurely movement, focused her camera and began taking some shots of the girl, catching her animated expression now that she was talking of Bill and their planned future. Sally looked self-conscious at first but then began to relax.

"Before and after," Casey explained as she focused and clicked the shutter. "These'll be fun to look at later."

Sally nodded, smiling. "Miss Logan—Casey—there's something I wanted to ask you. I know you've been staying with your aunt, Mrs. Pritchard. Is she coming to the wedding, by the way?"

"Yes, indeed. A friend is bringing her."

"Oh, good. Well...in the paper yesterday I saw an ad for a cottage, and it sounded to me like the one at Mrs. Pritchard's place. Dad heard you'd been fixing it up to rent. Is it taken yet?"

Casey shook her head. "We had a couple of calls last evening, but no. Nobody's even come to see it yet."

"Well, I was wondering, if the rent's anywhere near what Bill and I could manage, would you and your aunt consider renting it to us? Both of us work, but we've put all our savings into the business. It takes a while to get a new company started, so if we could find someplace nice with a reasonable rent..."

Casey smiled at her. "I'm sure Constance would be thrilled."

"You see," the girl hurried on. "Our parents are concerned because of Bill's being away a lot, too. They want us to stay with one of them at first. Bill's parents have a pretty good-size house, plenty of room, but the thing is, both Bill and I would rather have a place of our own."

Casey thought of the little cottage with its fireplace, its soft green walls, its polished old furniture and mullioned windows. "It isn't fancy," she said honestly. "But it's...well, it's the kind of place I'd like if I were getting married."

"Really?" Sally Ridley's eyes shone. "I just knew it somehow. When I read that ad I couldn't help thinking it might be for us."

A bittersweet pain lodged somewhere in Casey's chest as she thought of what the cottage meant to her. She forced herself to return to practical considerations.

"You wouldn't be all alone, either," she said encouragingly. "My aunt's right there, and the Townsends are across the road." It would be good for Constance, too, she was thinking. Sturdy, practical Sally with her sunny disposition would be an ideal tenant. "I'm afraid there isn't time to show it to you before the ceremony, but perhaps you could see it afterward. Are you going away on a wedding trip?"

"Yes, but not far. Only up to the Adirondacks for a couple of days."

"Maybe you could stop in on your way." Casey explained where the key hung. "Let yourselves in and have a look before you go."

"Wonderful! I'll see you about it as soon as we get back," Sally promised, her eyes bright with conspiracy.

"All right, now," Tess Ridley said, bustling back from the kitchen, cheeks pinker than ever. "Only an hour till the ceremony. Let's start getting you ready. Where's Linda?"

"On her way, I'm sure," Sally said soothingly. "Maid of honor," she explained to Casey. "We graduated from high school together. And grade school," she added. "She's going to dress here with me."

"Go ahead." Casey waved them off up the stairs. "I'll hang around and take some more shots. When you're just about ready, call me. Everybody dressed and putting on the last-minute touches, that sort of thing."

"Okay." Sally bounded up the steps, looking like a high-school girl herself, and Tess plodded after, out of breath and fanning herself with her apron.

CASEY HAD OFTEN BEEN instructed by her clients in Washington to take pictures of the actual ceremony, but today, in the small whitewashed sanctuary of the tree-shaded church, she watched quietly from a pew near the back and kept her camera in its case as the young couple made their vows at the altar. A photographer, however tactful, would have been an intrusion, she thought. Her eyes darted repeatedly through the crowd looking for Travis, and she felt a plunging disappointment when she failed to catch sight of his tall figure. But there could be a dozen reasons for that, she told herself sensibly. He had said he'd see her at the wedding, and of course he would, if not at the church, then at the Ridleys' house later. A doctor's time wasn't always his own, and Barker Springs wasn't like a big city, where another doctor could take over as a convenience or a courtesy. Here there was no other doctor, and if something unexpected came up, some sort of medical emergency, of course he would be detained. She noticed Constance, sitting halfway back in the church with Dr. Leland Somers on one side, Leo and Anna Bates on the other. She saw other familiar faces, too, people she'd come to know these past few weeks. No sign of Lee Nelson, but that didn't really mean anything, she reassured herself quickly, forcing down a sudden uneasy feeling. She watched the nervous young bridegroom put the ring on Sally's finger, saw them kiss and then turn to walk back up the aisle, smiling and dewy-eyed. Casey slipped outside and waited on the steps for a shot of the emerging wedding party.

From then on, the afternoon slid into a haze of happy confusion as bridal party and guests all returned to the Ridley home. Because the afternoon had turned out picture-perfect, the reception was held on the broad lawn behind the house and there was plenty of room for everyone. Under huge old maple trees, tables had been set up to hold the food; chairs were scattered about so that those who wanted to could sit. Laughter and kissing, exclamations and an occasional tear mingled and blended in Casey's impressions. She moved easily among the guests, concentrating on her work, focusing, setting up shots, catching the guests as they talked, ate, greeted friends. At one point she saw Sally, standing near the laden table with her new husband at her side. They were gazing deep into each other's eyes when a vagrant breeze came along, catching the bridal veil and tossing it back so that it billowed out behind Sally like a cloud. Casey focused and shot quickly, capturing the moment.

"Where in the world is Travis?" Constance asked, leaning on her cane but looking remarkably well and rather dramatic in a long, loose dress of dark sea-green. A pale, lace scarf was thrown around her shoulders, and her usually flyaway hair was brushed into a low coil.

"I don't know. I suppose something detained him." Casey busied herself with her camera, fussing with the lens opening. She'd been watching for Travis ever since they'd arrived at the house. "Doesn't Leland know?"

Constance's gaze turned to where Leland was greeting the bride with his customary gallantry. "He says he doesn't. They were at the hospital together this morning. That was the last he saw of him, he says."

Casey took a shot of Leland as he leaned close to speak to Sally and shake hands with Bill. "I'm sure he'll be along soon," she said, but her hands were beginning to feel chilly in the warm summer afternoon, and she fumbled awkwardly with the camera. Once again she glanced across the lawn toward the house, and suddenly there was Travis, standing with one hand in his pocket, looking around.

"He's just arrived," Casey whispered exultantly. "Excuse me, Constance." Her heart had begun to pound with joy as she hurried, smiling, across the grass toward him. Halfway there she realized something was wrong; something in his posture and attitude was unfamiliar. He stood rigidly straight, chin lifted slightly, and scanned the crowd with narrowed eyes. When she reached him, she could see that the blue eyes were as coldly gray as seawater.

"Travis! We wondered when you were coming," she said eagerly, but when he looked at her he seemed scarcely to see her. His brows drew together in a frown.

"Is Lee here?" he asked. "Has anyone seen her?"

"Lee!" Casey echoed the name stupidly, not understanding.

"Yes. Was she at the church?" he demanded.

"I didn't see her. No, I don't think she was," Casey said, trying to keep her voice normal, but feeling a tight knot of disappointment inside her. Her words sounded distant in her own ears. Like someone else's words, coming from faraway.

"Casey!" Someone called to her from across the lawn, from the table where a tall, white wedding cake was being brought in and placed before the bridal couple.

"Excuse me," she said in a small, pinched voice. "I have to get a shot of this." He didn't answer.

Moments later, when she turned back to where he'd been standing, she was just in time to see him walk toward someone coming through the white picket gate. Lee Nelson, with a man Casey didn't recognize. Lee seemed to be introducing the two men, and after a moment moved aside with Travis as he bent and spoke to her. Casey edged enough to hear fragments of what they were saying. Hating herself for eavesdropping, she nevertheless could not help standing there, transfixed.

"He met me at the airport," she heard Lee say. "I didn't have my car with me.... No, that's all it was, really, Travis." Lee looked small and slender in a dress of aqua silk. Travis said something else, but his back was to Casey and she couldn't catch it. Lee put a hand on his arm and then Casey heard her say, "No, of course I didn't. How could you think a thing like that?" Her soft voice sounded pleading.

Casey turned away, blinded by tears, as cold as if a chilling north wind had suddenly swept over the summer-green lawn. She returned to the bridal party, now happily cutting and passing out wedding cake, and took shot after shot, focusing and clicking mechanically, performing actions she had done so often they were second nature. Once she became aware of Constance watching with an expression of concern, but Casey glanced away. She didn't look in Travis's direction again.

She finished her picture-taking as quickly as possible and said her goodbyes to the bride and groom, shrugging off their profuse thanks. Then she whispered in Constance's ear that she was leaving. Constance nodded, her eyes searching Casey's face, but she asked no questions, and Casey hurried out to her car without encountering Travis in the crowd again.

How could she have been so stupid? Casey shook her head angrily and forced herself to concentrate on her driving as she headed home. How could she have succumbed to the oldest deception in the book, mistaking passion for love, desire for sincerity? The dark anger on Travis's face when he saw Lee Nelson with another man was truer and more revealing than all that had been between them that night in the cottage. She'd been so critical of her life in Washington, the frivolity of it, the fact that her father had probably used his influence to get her the museum job she'd wanted. But was that kind of shallowness any worse than the deception she had experienced here? Achingly, she turned her thoughts away from the voice she had come to love as it spoke soft words to her in the dark. She forced herself to ignore her memories of the strong arms that had held her, the outpouring of her own love, so freely given. Gullible, foolish, trusting—she had been all of those and more.

It was late afternoon when Casey pulled into the driveway of her aunt's house. The grass, which she had raked and mowed and weeded, was beginning to take hold in the front yard. The pink impatiens Constance had planted around the porch were thriving and putting out fresh blossoms. There were still blooms left on the roses, and the purple clematis had started climbing over the porch railing, lavishly thick.

Casey stared at all of it with loving eyes, but seeing it dimly as tears welled up. She hurried inside to her room, where she changed quickly out of the silk dress, slipping into jeans and running shoes and a red-and-white-checked shirt. Then she pulled her suitcase out from under the bed and began packing.

She was finished here. Just when she'd begun to think that this place meant more to her than anyplace she'd ever lived, she was done with it. The cottage would be rented—she was sure of that. Bill and Sally Henderson would love it. And everything else was in order, the grounds tidy, most of the stray animals adopted. The others would be taken soon; she had left pictures with Joan Singleton for another pet column. Constance's bookkeeping was in order; Casey was quite certain her affairs had never been so well arranged. And now Constance had Leland, a new friend who'd come into her life. Even after he returned to New Hampshire, they would have each other. You could tell, somehow, when a thing was meant to last, Casey thought wistfully. What was it Constance had said to her? *Some things are just meant to be and others aren't.*

How could she have been so stupid? Why hadn't she been able to tell the difference?

She finished her packing, then stood for a moment in the middle of the room looking carefully around, as if to impress on her memory the worn flowered rug, the thin white curtains, the old-fashioned chest of drawers with its oval mirror. After that, she went downstairs and let Nick and Sarge out of the screened back porch. She'd decided to take them for a walk to the pond.

A last walk, she thought, but could not bear to say. "Come on, you two," she called to the dogs. "And you'll have to behave. No barking at beavers."

The dogs trotted obediently at her heels until they were halfway there, when the older, more sedate Sarge decided to turn around and go back home. She and Nick went on, across the fragrant meadow, now full of daisies and buttercups, toward the little stand of trees and the beaver pond.

She was fifty feet from the pond when she realized something was wrong. She could hear the ominous sound of rushing water. Feeling a jolt of panic, she broke into a run; the little dog galloped along with her, ears flying. Casey's heart was in her throat, and her chest burned with fear.

"Oh, no!" she cried, pulling up short at the pond and surveying the damage.

The five-foot dam of sticks and mud, sturdy and impenetrable to ordinary pressures, had been ripped open. A huge gap had been torn in the center of it, and water was gushing through the break and tearing away still more of the structure. The level of water in the pond was already visibly lower, although the underwater entrance to the beaver lodge wasn't in sight yet. But it wouldn't be long before it stood exposed to the world, and to predators. Casey thought of the little family crouching inside, fearful and confused, of the two kits whose growth she had watched. She looked around for something— anything—to throw into the breached dam, but she knew it would take more than her efforts to stop the flow. She must get to a telephone.

Yet even as she turned back and started running toward the house, doubts and uncertainties crowded in on her. Whom could she possibly call? The sheriff? Despite all his good intentions, Hank Beltzer wouldn't be the man to help in this kind of situation.

Then faintly, in the far distance, she heard the roar of motorcycles.

CHAPTER TEN

SHE SAW THE BLAZER pulling into the driveway as she approached the house, and for one paralyzed moment she simply stood there. Travis got out, still in the dark suit he'd been wearing at the reception. Observing his lean, muscular good looks, it occurred to her, with a strange irrelevance, that she had never seen him so dressed up before today.

He strode toward her. "Casey! Where did you disappear to? I asked Constance, and she said you'd just cut out."

Relief overrode all other emotions as Casey ran to him.

"Travis! Oh, thank heavens you're here. The beaver dam's broken. Water's pouring over it and the pond's going down."

"Broken?" he echoed, staring at her in disbelief.

"Someone did it deliberately, you can tell. We've got to try and stop the water." For the moment it didn't matter to her that everything had gone terribly wrong between them, that their relationship would never be the same again, that something had broken in her as surely as it had in the dam. All that mattered now was that they save the four animals she'd come to think of as friends.

Travis was already ahead of her, running across the meadow toward the water. Her heart pounding, her breath coming in hot gasps, Casey ran after him.

Travis took in the situation at a glance. Quickly he began picking up large rocks from the edge of the pond and throwing them into the breached dam. He was wading knee-deep in mud, and Casey, half-sobbing, followed his lead and began clawing at any rocks she could find and passing them to him.

"Not enough." He shook his head. "We need bigger ones."

"Sticks might help," she said, and flew to the pile she'd brought there a few days earlier. The beavers had been working on them, but some of them remained. She started dragging them to Travis, aware even as she did so that it was a pitifully small pile to stem the powerful rush of water streaming through the break.

"What'll happen to the beavers?" she gasped. "I mean, if the level keeps going down?"

He tossed another rock into the gap. The water swallowed it as if it had been a pebble. "If the lodge is exposed, they'll all be in danger. The kits especially. There are predators around—foxes, stray dogs—even a good-size hawk could make off with a kit. And of course people."

Casey's voice came out in a sob. "Oh, Travis, what can we do?"

Over the rush of water she again heard the roar of motorcycles. Travis heard it, too, and they both turned to see two bikes headed toward them across the field, two space-helmeted figures bent forward over the handlebars.

"Watch out!" Casey cried, but a few feet away from them the bikes came to a halt. The riders cut their motors, dismounted and walked toward them, two booted figures in torn jeans and leather jackets. The panic she'd been feeling about the dam changed to a chilling fear.

What else could possibly happen? Travis straightened and stood with his hands on his hips, confronting them. "Yes? What do you want? What are you doing here?"

"Looks like you've got some trouble." The biker's voice was muffled behind his helmet.

"Oh, for heaven's sake," Casey muttered through clenched teeth. "Of course they know there's trouble. They're the ones who—"

"Hold on a minute, Casey," Travis said. The bikers unfastened their helmets and slid them off. One of the men was dark-haired and short, the other red-haired and lanky. Both appeared to be in their twenties.

"You folks have a problem?" the red-haired man asked.

"We saw you running over here, looked like something had happened," the shorter one said. "Anything we can do?" The two faces were open and earnest. Not really menacing, Casey thought. Did she have this all wrong?

Travis was ahead of her. "The beaver dam's been vandalized," he said.

The bikers' gazes swung to the ragged break where the water was gushing through.

"Looks like somebody took a pickax to it," the red-head said.

Travis nodded gloomily. "At the rate the water's pouring out, it won't be long before the pond's dry."

"That's bad, huh?" the same man muttered.

"Yes, it is. Rocks are all we've got to use."

"Well, I'll be." The dark-haired man surveyed the damage. "Who'd do a thing like that?"

His lanky cohort was already leaning over, heaving a large rock from the bank of the pond. The shorter man joined him, both of them struggling with their burdens, lugging them over to the dam, tossing them into the breach. Casey shook her head unbelievingly. *Make a note, Casey Logan,* she told herself sternly. *No more snap judgments about a person's character.*

They worked steadily, the men picking up the larger rocks and throwing them into the gaping hole, Casey lining up smaller ones to help fill in. Eventually all four of them were muddied beyond recognition, wet and soaked with sweat. The sun began to sink lower, and dusk slowly settled around them.

At last Travis said helplessly, "It's not working. We may have slowed the water a little, but it's still pouring over."

"But we can't give up!" Casey exclaimed. "We've got to keep at it."

"It's hopeless. Water's leaking through those rocks like a sieve," Travis muttered, but he reached for another one. She could see the muscles of his shoulders strain under his wet shirt. He had thrown his coat onto the ground. For the nearest fraction of a second Casey remembered how the strength of that body had felt holding her in the night, how she'd longed to be held like that forever, close and safe.

From across the pond came a faint splash, and Casey looked startled. She could see a familiar V-shape in the water. A beaver had left the lodge and was now swimming toward the break, its caution regarding humans set aside in the moment of crisis. It was undoubtedly the big male. Casey had come to recognize them all by now. He seemed to survey the deadly break in the dam, his small eyes full of alarm. Then, instinct and intelligence working quickly, he swam to the far shore and began felling a sapling with his chisel-sharp teeth. It was, for Casey, even sadder than the moment of finding the broken dam. Her mind suddenly formed a picture, like the image in a camera's viewfinder, of the four humans and their puny efforts, the indomitable animal and his dogged attempt to stem a tide that was beyond all of them, raging and unstoppable. By morning, she knew, the pond would be dry. And would the little family stay alive long enough to build another dam? She caught Travis looking at her, and thought what she must look like, mud-smeared and sweaty, her hair coming loose from its braid.

"We can't do any more," he said quietly. "We're running out of rocks, for one thing. Forget it. And thanks a lot, guys."

The two bikers stood, panting and soaked, surveying the damage. "Damn," the short one said. "Doggone it all. That's a shame."

"Won't you come back to the house for coffee?" Casey asked wearily. "You were so good to help."

"No, shoot, that's all right. Glad to do it," the redhead said. "My name's Waldo, by the way. This here's Bert. We work over to Pat's Body Shop on Route 50." Damp and muddy handshakes were exchanged all around. "We'll be getting along now. Sure am sorry we couldn't save it. Come on, Bert."

Casey and Travis watched and waved as the two took off, roaring away across the field.

"So much for my ability to judge character," Casey said, trying to summon up a small smile, but feeling it defeated by the utter hopelessness that washed over her. And suddenly it was more than just the beaver dam and their failure to save it. Memory came rushing back, and with it all the hurt she'd experienced at the wedding reception. For this brief time it had been pushed back by a greater urgency, but now it welled up again like a flood, engulfing and smothering her.

A light was on in the house.

"Constance must be home," she said. "I'd better go tell her about this."

"I'll come with you."

"No." She said it so quickly that he gave her an odd look. "I'd rather speak to her myself."

"Okay." He studied her in the dusky light. "For whatever good it'll do, I'll go report this to Hank Beltzer."

"Fine," she said curtly, and headed toward the back door. She was almost there when she heard his car start. The thought came to her then that the dam wasn't the only thing that had been destroyed that day.

"BUT WHY WOULD ANYONE do such a thing?" Constance said bleakly when Casey broke the news to her.

Casey could only shake her head helplessly.

"It isn't random violence, though, is it?" Constance mused. She was sitting at the kitchen table, still in her best dress and shawl, but something in her look had changed since she'd learned of this latest vandalism. Something had crumpled, some light had gone out of her eyes.

"No," Casey said carefully. "It certainly seems to be more than that." She gave her aunt a desperate smile. "We'll go out there tomorrow, see if the beavers made it through the night, and if they did, maybe we can rescue them somehow. After all, you rescued Walter."

"Walter was a kit, and injured," Constance said. "This is different. You can't rescue wild animals that easily." She got up wearily from the table, reached for her cane and started limping toward the door. For the first time since her arrival, it seemed to Casey that her aunt had lost some of her proud, stubborn feistiness. There was a look of defeat in the slump of her shoulders. At the door she turned back.

"You know, Casey, I've been thinking. Maybe it isn't such a good idea, my trying to hang on to this old place. I mean, maybe the sensible thing would be for me to just—"

"No!" Casey interrupted her forcefully. "No, don't decide anything tonight, Constance. Just wait. Wait till tomorrow and then we'll talk about it." She could not bear, suddenly, to hear her aunt say she might be better off with her sister in Short Hills.

"Yes. Well, all right," Constance said with a little wave of her free hand. "We'll talk tomorrow." She turned and then paused again. "Leland's leaving early in the morning," she said.

"But he'll be back—you know he will," Casey said, trying to sound upbeat.

"Oh, yes, I suppose so." Constance's voice drifted off uncertainly as she left the kitchen.

Casey soaked in the tub for almost an hour before going to bed. The hot water eased her tired muscles, but the relaxation that should have come eluded her. By the time she moved her suitcase off the bed and crawled between the worn sheets, her mood was so dark and discouraged she could only lie there tensely. Her stomach was knotted with anxiety, her throat felt so tight she had trouble swallowing. Everything she thought had changed for the better had suddenly fallen back into its old pattern of precarious balance. All the optimism was gone, the planning for the future that had brightened Constance's eyes and given her back a sense of will and purpose. And as for Travis... Constance turned her head into her pillow and tried to shut out thoughts of him. She could still see, behind her closed eyelids, how he had leaned over Lee Nelson, all his attention focused on her—obviously she'd been the only woman there as far as he was concerned. No one had to interpret that look for her. So much for Casey Logan and *her* plans for the future, she thought wretchedly. So much for hope and love and trust, three traitors she would take care to avoid in the future.

She willed herself into concentrating on Constance's problems again, going over and over the events that had led up to today—the vandalism, the fire, the destruction of the dam—all of them directed at Constance. But nothing untied the snarls, nothing eased the tension that resolved itself finally into a pounding, throbbing headache. Finally she got up, fumbled her way to the bathroom and took a couple of aspirin. When she returned to bed she fell asleep at last, but she slept poorly. She dreamed of beavers, and all night long seemed to hear small voices murmuring pleas for help....

She was surprised, when she made her way down to the kitchen the next morning, to find Constance respectably dressed and sitting at the table. Casey's eyes widened with surprise.

"Church," Constance announced. "I'm going to church. That is, if you'll drive me. I don't think I'm up to handling that old truck yet."

"Of course I'll drive you. Maybe church would do us both good. Only I'd like to take a quick walk out to the dam first."

It pained Casey to see that the old fire no longer snapped in her aunt's dark eyes. "Don't," Constance said, resignation weighting her voice. "After church will be time enough."

"But—"

"There's nothing any of us can do, Casey. You did everything you could last night. If the beavers survive, they'll move on to some other place. If they don't, well . . . let nature handle it."

Casey poured herself a cup of coffee and drank it slowly.

"All right," she said quietly. "I'll get ready."

THE CHURCH WHERE they'd attended the wedding the day before was cheerful with some of the leftover floral arrangements, and Casey decided it had been a wise move, coming to the Sunday-morning service. Neighbors were greeting each other and were happy to see Constance, and Casey thought her aunt looked a little less defeated. Casey's own attention kept wandering, no matter how she tried to concentrate on the service. But the sound of the old hymns and the minister's steady voice as he spoke of eternal truths, washed over her in a soothing way, stilling some of the feverish doubts and anxieties that whirled around in her head. Harmony, she thought, letting her eyelids close. There was a kind of peaceful harmony here.

Casey's eyes flew open. Harmony. Something clicked in her brain as she racked through it for a shred of memory. Not harmony, that wasn't it, not exactly. She waited for the minister's benediction, then whispered to Constance, "I'll see you outside. There's someone I have to speak to."

She had already spotted Joan Singleton and her husband on the other side of the church. Now she followed them out and caught up with them at the foot of the church steps. She greeted them both hastily, then asked, "Joan, what was that man's name?"

"Hi, Casey." Joan seemed to take her abruptness in stride. "What man?"

"The one who wants to build a factory here."

"Oh, it's—what is it, Ed?" She turned to her husband.

"Harmon, isn't it?"

"I knew it," Casey breathed. "How do you suppose I could reach him?"

"Well, he lives downstate somewhere, near New York, I think. Maybe Long Island. Wait a minute." Joan opened a roomy handbag and rummaged through it. "Here. My notebook may have something..." She fished it out, explaining, "I covered that last meeting of the town board myself because I knew they'd be discussing it. Here it is. I got his number, thinking I might want to call him later for a statement. What's up? If it's a story, don't forget to tell me about it."

Casey was copying the number furiously. "You bet I will," she promised. "And thanks, Joan. Thanks, Ed."

She glanced up at the church, where Constance was just shaking hands with the pastor. Casey waited impatiently for her to come down the steps, flanked by Anna and Leo Bates.

"We're invited to Sunday dinner," Constance called out. "How's that for a stroke of luck? I've been doing so much socializing this week I hardly know myself." She seemed to be making a deliberate effort to sound cheerful.

"Sounds great, but you go on without me," Casey said hurriedly. "There's something I have to do."

Constance's eyes were troubled again. "Casey, if it's about the beavers, don't wear yourself out trying to..."

Casey shook her head, closing her eyes firmly for a moment.

"Don't worry about me," she said. "It's just...there are some things I have to see about."

Constance studied her worriedly, but Leo Bates took over in his hearty way. "Well now, if there's something she has to do, let her do it, Constance. And don't worry about this lady," he told Casey. "We'll bring her home later."

Casey thanked them and hurried off, across the street and down the block to the drugstore, where she knew there was a public telephone. She dashed in and made her call. She spoke for several minutes, and when she'd hung up, consulted the telephone book dangling from a chain nearby.

"Can you tell me where Poplar Lane is?" she asked the girl at the cash register.

"Sure. It's where those new houses are. Just go past the church and the library and take the first right."

Casey thanked her and strode back outside, hurrying to her car, parked under a big maple near the church. A few of the congregation still lingered, chatting, on the front lawn. She drove down the street and took the first right, finding herself in a newer section of town. All the trees were smaller and seemed to be newly planted, and the houses were smart and glossy. Casey slowed down to look for numbers. Number fifteen was at the end of the street, a house that backed into a wooded area and glittered with large windows and sliding glass doors. She turned into the driveway and got out of the car, then walked up the front steps and rang the bell at a big double-doored entrance.

After a moment she heard footsteps from inside, and Lee Nelson opened the door. Her face held a look of total surprise. She was wearing slacks and a long, loose overblouse in deep rose silk. Her feet were thrust into backless gold-colored sandals. Her dark hair swung silkily around her ears as she pulled the door wide.

"Casey! For goodness' sake—come on in."

The interior matched the outside of the house, Casey thought. Oversize couches, long-necked floor lamps, glass coffee tables, splashy contemporary paintings on the walls.

"What brings you out on a Sunday morning?" Lee asked. "How about some coffee?"

Casey shook her head. "I wanted to let you know, Lee. I just talked with Mr. Harmon in Long Island."

The cordiality left Lee's face. Her dark eyes turned wary, and her mouth tilted downward at the corners, sullen and evasive.

"Oh, really? What on earth for?"

Casey didn't answer directly. "He's made a decision on which property he wants to buy here in Barker Springs." She hesitated. "He's buying the original tract he looked at, the one over on the Addison Mills road. He's decided not to buy my aunt's property."

Color flared in Lee's face, then faded to paleness. "Well, of course not. Your aunt's property isn't for sale, is it?" she asked crisply.

Casey, who was standing just inside the living-room archway, realized her hands were balled into tight fists. She let her fingers relax a little.

"No. And that's the point, isn't it? If you'd been successful in frightening her into selling, you'd have made him a good deal and yourself a hefty profit."

"I haven't the faintest idea what you're talking about." Lee whirled around, went to the coffee table and reached for a cigarette.

"Oh, I think you do. Vandalism, starting fires—"

Lee blew out smoke angrily. "You certainly don't think I did any of that!"

"I'm sure you know who did." Casey began to feel more relaxed, sure of her ground. "I knew it had to be something bigger than just a routine local real-estate deal. You told me about Henry Harmon wanting to locate his company here." She paused, watching Lee closely, then continued in a calm, quiet voice. "I know it's not uncommon for a firm to look at more than one site before they buy. My aunt has twenty-five acres there. It would certainly be desirable. Also, that property on the Addison Mills road wasn't one of your firm's listings, was it?"

Lee deliberately ignored the question. "And so you had the brilliant idea of calling Harmon. Well, what does that prove?" Her face had drawn itself into a look of scorn.

"Only that he confirmed what I'd suspected. He said you'd told him about twenty-five acres that would be on the market soon. You said you could get it for him at a good price. Only he's decided not to wait, but to go ahead and buy the original piece he'd looked at."

Lee paced to the big window beyond which the little woods lay, glanced out, then whirled around again.

"You needn't think anyone in town will believe you," she snapped. "All those wild accusations about vandalism and arson. I've lived here all my life. Who's going to listen to you? Do you think we're all impressed because you're Senator Logan's daughter? You're so desperate to get Travis Grant you'd say anything just to get me out of the picture."

"Travis has nothing to do with this," Casey retorted hotly. "Whatever's between you two doesn't interest me in the least. I couldn't care less. But I do care about my aunt and what happens to her.''

''This is the wildest, most irresponsible talk I've ever heard.''

Casey said coolly, ''I was never more sure of anything in my life.''

Lee walked to the table and crushed out her cigarette. Then she stood with her arms folded, hands clasping her elbows, and confronted Casey.

''Well, you can't prove it, can you?'' she said. Her voice was tight with mockery.

Casey felt her heart plummet and a cold emptiness fill her as she realized the truth of what Lee was saying. How could she possibly prove it?

There was the soft sound of a footstep behind her and a voice said, ''No. You can't, can you, Casey?''

Casey's hand flew to her throat as she twisted around. Travis was standing there in the archway, the front door still open behind him. He was dressed as she'd so often seen him, in a white shirt and faded jeans. In spite of the shock, she could not control her body's initial reaction to him—the quickened pulse, the flush of longing. His eyes flickered from her to Lee, and there was a hint of a smile on his face. Everything in Casey cried out silently in denial. He couldn't possibly be in on this with Lee. He couldn't be!

''No, I don't think you'd have an easy time proving it, Casey.'' He looked back at her, then said with slow deliberation, ''But I can.'' His expression unreadable, he took a step into the room, and his glance went from one to the other. ''And so can Marv Butler, who spent a good part of last night spilling the whole story to Sheriff Beltzer.''

"Travis!" Lee hurried to his side and gazed up at him pleadingly. "For heaven's sake, you certainly aren't taking the word of the town drunk about something like this, are you? How can you possibly think that of me?"

Travis gave her a look of such intensity that Casey could only watch in utter confusion.

"Honey," he said softly, "I've thought that about you since the day I moved here." His eyes sought out Casey. "Let's go, shall we?"

CHAPTER ELEVEN

THE TWO OF THEM sat at the table in Constance's kitchen. Sunlight glinted off the spoons that stood in the glass tumbler in the middle of the table. Outside, blue jays squawked noisily in the pine tree near the house.

"How did you know?" Casey asked in a small voice. She sat across the table from him, wanting to keep her distance, unsure of what was between them now.

"Same way you did." He spread both hands, palms up, and it was all Casey could do to keep from putting out her own hand to touch him.

"You mean through Mr. Harmon?" She took a sip of coffee, willing herself to be calm.

He nodded. "Except that he called me. Yesterday morning. He knew I was interested in his plans, and actually we'd gotten along well the times I'd seen him. He knew I was concerned about the impact of his factory on the town. Said he wanted to let me know he was going to buy the original plot of land he'd looked at. He'd decided he wasn't interested in the other twenty-five acres he'd been offered."

Casey's breath caught in a quick gasp.

He gave her a wry smile. "Yes, that was my reaction. I had no idea he was considering any other location. He explained that it had been described to him as a very desirable piece of land and he'd received a pledge that it would be on the market at any moment. However, he liked the original parcel and decided to go with that. He was going to announce it officially on Monday, but he called me as a courtesy.''

"He must have been thoroughly confused when I telephoned him with my questions,'' Casey said, smiling.

"Well, it didn't take much to realize it was Constance's property he was talking about. And since I knew Constance didn't want to sell, I figured it could only mean that Lee had made the offer. And the vandalism, the fire, even the destruction of the dam, were all designed to push Constance into a decision. Her circumstances were precarious, anyway—Lee knew that.''

"So from there it was just a matter of figuring out who in town would do such things for hire?''

They looked at each other across the table and said in one voice, "Marv Butler.''

"Sheriff Beltzer isn't any world-beater as a lawman,'' Travis went on, "but even he got suspicious when he saw Marv spending money in grand style in a bar outside of town. Hauled him in for disturbing the peace, which Marv does pretty regularly, anyway, and the whole story came out. I stopped in to talk to the sheriff when I left here last night and caught the whole show.''

Casey moved her finger slowly around the rim of her cup. "But you already knew it was Lee.''

He nodded. "I was sure of it.''

"And at the wedding reception yesterday...''

Two lines appeared in his forehead as he frowned in recollection. "Ah, yes. The reception. I'm afraid I missed most of it. I had this thing on my mind, you see, and I couldn't wait to confront Lee with it. I tried reaching her by phone first, but her answering machine said she was out of town. I figured she might show up for the wedding, though. Lee never likes to miss a crowd scene. She does a lot of business that way. So when I saw her come in I immediately asked her about it.''

"That man she was with—who was he?" Casey asked.

"Oh, that was Howard Kendall. He's a big builder around here who's pretty tight with Lee. I imagine he was angling for the contract to build Harmon's factory. The two of them with their heads together like that didn't please me too much, either.''

"You accused her of being responsible for all the trouble at Constance's?"

He nodded. "I'm afraid I sailed right into her—I was so worked up by that time."

In her mind Casey heard again Lee's words—*No, of course I didn't. How could you think a thing like that?* She closed her eyes for a moment, shaking her head slowly as she realized that once again she had leapt to a conclusion on insufficient evidence.

"I thought..." she began. She stopped and tried again, but no matter how she rephrased it, she still felt foolish and petty. "You looked so concerned about her. And you seemed angry that she'd come with another man. I thought you were having a lovers' quarrel."

For a moment he stared at her, blue eyes wide with astonishment. "Was *that* what made you go flying home? I couldn't imagine. I was looking everywhere, because I wanted to tell you what I'd found out. Of course I didn't know about the beaver dam then, but later when I wanted to come in and talk to you about it— and Constance, too—you turned your back on me and walked away, mad as a hornet." He got up suddenly, almost knocking his chair over. He came around the table, urged her to her feet and suddenly enveloped her in his arms, pulling her close to him and holding her so tight that Casey felt herself melting away, as if her very bones were dissolving. He tipped her head up and kissed her long and hard. Then he stepped back and looked down at her, shaking his head gently.

"Casey, how could you think that? How could you think for one minute that I'd . . ."

She shook her head desperately, not trusting herself to speak, then reached up and drew his head down to her again. For a long moment they stood there clinging to each other. At last Casey found her voice. Resting her head against his chest, listening to the steady beat of his heart, she said, "We have to go out there, you know."

His hand moved caressingly over her back. "Out where?"

"We have to see what happened to them." She raised her face to him, feeling such exultation that she wanted nothing to intrude on this moment. But she knew they had to return to the pond.

"The beavers."

She nodded. "Constance says it's hard to rescue wild things, but we've got to see, haven't we? If any of them survived?"

He kissed her again. "I don't think I'd love you if you weren't the sort of woman who worried about beavers at a time like this." He grinned. "Come on."

They walked across the meadow hand in hand. As they neared the pond site there was an ominous quiet that made Casey glance up at him anxiously. "It's all over, isn't it? All the water's drained out. I don't hear a thing."

"I'm afraid so."

"What will they do?"

"If they survive, they'll move to another place, build another dam. We'll hope they don't decide on a spot too near a state highway—or unsympathetic people."

They quickened their pace and covered the distance to the pond. When they reached the bank they stood and stared.

Instead of the gaping hole they'd last seen with the stream gushing through it and emptying the pond, they saw a structure that seemed to comprise every kind of material imaginable. Branches of all sizes, small sticks, twigs had all been plugged into the gap, stuck every which way into the bed of stones Travis, Casey and the bikers had thrown down in desperate haste. Some of the twigs bore blossoms, giving the structure a rakish, holiday look, and in the cracks were mud, weeds, leaves, even a few daylilies, roots and all, their orange blooms riding triumphantly above the water. In one spot a plastic bag that must have caught on the reeds at the edge of the water had been used as a plug.

"I don't believe it," Travis breathed softly. "They did it. We couldn't fix it, but they did."

"We helped," Casey said, observing it through her tears. The level of the water, lower than normal, was nevertheless rising, and the underwater entrance to the lodge was still concealed.

"Look," Travis said suddenly. "Over there."

Casey followed his pointing finger. A beaver had just emerged from the lodge and was swimming purposefully toward the end of the pond. A second one followed him.

"Mr. and Mrs.," she whispered, and Travis nodded. The two approached the ridiculous-looking dam, edged along it, nosed it professionally, then swam away as if satisfied. Travis's arm came around Casey, pulling her close.

"Katharine Case Logan," he murmured. "Have I mentioned that I love you?"

"I think we covered that, but you could say it again." She turned her face up to his and drank in his kisses hungrily.

The telephone was ringing when they finally got back to the house.

"Maybe it's Constance," Casey said. "Wait till she hears." She hurried to the front hall to answer.

"Katharine?" The familiar voice, slightly impatient, imperious, no longer caused her heart to drop with dismay.

"Hello, Dad." She smiled at Travis as he came to stand beside her.

"What's going on there, for heaven's sake? I've been waiting to hear from you, and Harrison Bentley says he wasn't able to reach you. What about the property? And what about this photography show? Are you coming to do it or not? Really, Katharine, I think you could behave a little more responsibly."

"Hold on, Dad. You have no idea how responsibly I'm behaving." She smiled at Travis and spoke into the telephone again. "I've written to Mr. Bentley telling him when I'll be there. That's all set and my suitcase is packed." She'd packed it when she had planned to run away from Travis, but no need to explain that, she thought. "As far as the property is concerned, Aunt Constance has decided not to sell. She's renting out the cottage she owns, and she'll have enough to get along. She's already got tenants for it." Travis's eyebrows went up in a question, and Casey made a circle of her thumb and index finger to confirm it.

"But she's on crutches. She's sick, she's old—"

"She's not on crutches any longer. She's not sick, and she acts younger than you do." Casey took a deep breath and said contritely, "No, Dad, I didn't mean that. But she'll be fine. And she wants to stay right here." She paused, then added, "I'll be staying, too."

There was a silence at the other end of the line. "You'll be staying? But what about the show here in Washington?"

"I'll come for that, and maybe if Mr. Bentley likes my work I'll come back for others. But this is where I'm going to be living." Putting it into words suddenly made it a reality. Again she heard dead silence on the line. "I have a new career in mind," Casey told her father. "I'm going to be renovating some of these old country places here and renting or selling them. I think it's a good market. Look, Dad, why don't I call you later today and tell you more about it? Love to Mother."

She hung up and turned to Travis, who was grinning at her and shaking his head. "I'll bet Senator Logan doesn't get talked to that way very often."

"It probably did him good."

"What's this about a new career? And is your suitcase really packed?"

"It's something I've been thinking a lot about. And it ties in with my other work—I mean, taking before and after pictures. Oh, I know all I did in the cottage was some painting and cleaning. But I'm absolutely sure I can do it. I'll be learning as I go along, and I'll ask Leo Bates to help me with things I need to know. And yes, I do have to get back," she said reluctantly. "I've promised to do that exhibition."

"I'll miss you." His eyes lingered on her. "How soon will you be back?"

"In a few weeks. But I hope to see you before that."

"What do you mean?"

Casey leaned over and picked up a portfolio she'd stuck behind the telephone stand. "I have something to show you." She opened it and brought out the pictures she'd taken of Constance. "They'll be in the exhibition in Washington. I want her to see them."

He looked them over admiringly. "Hey, you really are good."

She flushed with pleasure. "Will you do it? Will you come to the show and bring Constance?"

"You can count on it. I wouldn't miss it."

There was the sound of a car door slamming outside, and Casey put the pictures away quickly as Constance came up the steps and in the front door. She was balancing a foil-wrapped dish in one hand.

She glanced from one to the other without surprise. "All right, what about the beavers? You've been out there?"

"They're safe, Constance. They finished plugging the dam themselves after we gave up and left."

Casey could see the wave of relief that washed over the older woman's face, although she controlled it quickly. "Well, I don't wonder at it. Enterprising animals, beavers." She started walking back toward the kitchen, leaning on her cane, but her step was already visibly lighter. "Either of you have anything to eat? Anna made me bring home the leftovers—chicken and biscuits with gravy. Come along, come along. I want to hear all about this. Any idea who's responsible?"

Quickly and without wasting words, Travis told her about Lee Nelson. Constance listened quietly, showing only faint surprise, her expressive face mirroring a philosophical acceptance of the world's shortcomings. Then she shook her head. "What's going to happen to her?"

"Well, unless you press charges—"

"Oh, no, no. Nothing like that." Constance waved the idea away.

"Well, it's going to come out, anyway. Marv Butler's told the sheriff, so the whole town will know. I imagine she'll lose her real-estate license."

Constance began preparing plates for them, looking up now and then, her dark eyes probing. Travis and Casey sat at the table, this time close together, their hands locked under it.

"When will you be leaving?" she asked Casey. "Saw your suitcase when I went by your door."

"Maybe I packed too soon," Casey said. "But I do have to be in Washington by Friday."

Constance frowned thoughtfully. "Doesn't give you much time, does it?"

"Time for what?"

Travis grinned. "For us to get married, of course."

Casey turned to him, staring into his eyes. *Married.* Her lips formed the word soundlessly as his arm came around her, pulling her even closer. She felt the enveloping warmth of his body, the strength of the arm that held her. From the hollow of his shoulder she murmured happily, "Plenty of time, I'd say."

"Well, then," Constance said dryly as she turned away from them and started filling the teakettle. "I might as well make some tea."

HARLEQUIN ROMANCE®

**Harlequin Romance
knows love can be dangerous!**

Don't miss
TO LOVE AND PROTECT (#3223)
by Kate Denton,
the October title in

THE BRIDAL COLLECTION

THE GROOM'S life was in peril.
THE BRIDE was hired to help him.
BUT THEIR WEDDING was *more* than
a business arrangement!

Available this month in
The Bridal Collection
JACK OF HEARTS (#3218)
by Heather Allison
Wherever Harlequin books are sold.

HARLEQUIN PRESENTS®

BARBARY WHARF

**An exciting six-book series, one title per month
beginning in October, by bestselling author**

Charlotte Lamb

Set in the glamorous and fast-paced world of international
journalism, BARBARY WHARF will take you from the
Sentinel's hectic newsroom to the most thrilling cities in the
world. You'll meet media tycoon Nick Caspian and his
adversary Gina Tyrrell, whose dramatic story of passion and
heartache develops throughout the six-book series.

In book one, BESIEGED (#1498), you'll also meet Hazel and
Piet. Hazel's always had a good word to say about everyone.
Well, almost. She just can't stand Piet Van Leyden, Nick's
chief architect and one of the most arrogant know-it-alls she's
ever met! As far as Hazel's concerned, Piet's a twentieth-
century warrior, and she's the one being besieged!

Don't miss the sparks in the first BARBARY WHARF
book, BESIEGED (#1498), available in October from
Harlequin Presents.